He Pulled Her into His Arms.

"If you pack a picnic lunch tomorrow, I'll bring the wine." His warm breath fanned her cheek as he spoke.

"Is that a request or an order?" Lisa asked breathlessly.

"I'll make it an order. Then I know you'll do it." He was unabashed. "You always follow my orders."

"So far," she teased.

Dan pressed a hard kiss against her lips. "Be ready at nine."

Then he was gone, and it was only later that Lisa wondered where the hard, arrogant Dan of the office had been tonight.

LINDA WISDOM
counts writing chief among her many interests. The world of the imagination has always been real to her, and with her novels she is able to bring everyone's dreams of love and romance to life.

Dear Reader:

Silhouette Romances is an exciting new publishing venture. We will be presenting the very finest writers of contemporary romantic fiction as well as outstanding new talent in this field. It is our hope that our stories, our heroes and our heroines will give you, the reader, all you want from romantic fiction.

Also, *you* play an important part in our future plans for Silhouette Romances. We welcome any suggestions or comments on our books and I invite you to write to us at the address below.

So, enjoy this book and all the wonderful romances from Silhouette. They're for *you!*

Karen Solem
Editor-in-Chief
Silhouette Books
P.O. Box 769
New York, N.Y. 10019

LINDA WISDOM
Bright Tomorrow

Silhouette *Romance*

Published by Silhouette Books New York

America's Publisher of Contemporary Romance

Other Silhouette Books by Linda Wisdom

Dancer in the Shadows
Fourteen Karat Beauty

SILHOUETTE BOOKS, a Simon & Schuster Division of
GULF & WESTERN CORPORATION
1230 Avenue of the Americas, New York, N.Y. 10020

Copyright © 1982 by Linda Wisdom

Distributed by Pocket Books

ISBN: 0-671-57132-X

First Silhouette Books printing February, 1982

10 9 8 7 6 5 4 3 2 1

Map by Tony Ferrara

America's Publisher of Contemporary Romance

Printed in the U.S.A.

To Diane, for all her help in bringing this book to life

Bright
Tomorrow

Chapter One

"It isn't fair, Mark," Lisa Winters argued with her boss on Friday afternoon. "Why me? There are other secretaries here who are just as capable as I am, if not more so. From everything I've heard about Dan Nolan, he's the last man I'd want to work for. He thinks he's a media star, not a lawyer."

"I realize this is unexpected, Lisa," Mark said heavily. "But having Dan Nolan come into the firm is very important to us. It was decided at a meeting of the senior partners that you would best fill the bill as his secretary. This change will also include a handsome raise for you." He dangled this last bit in front of her.

Mark Connors stood up, stretching tiredly. He was a man in his mid-forties, and his dark hair was liberally sprinkled with gray, giving him a distinguished air. His dark brown eyes took in the young woman seated across from him. Her shoulder-length hair, the shade of golden fire, and her liquid emerald eyes could not be viewed without interest by any man. In the eighteen months Lisa had been his secretary, Mark had come to see her as more than just someone to grace his front office and carry out routine duties.

"There's another reason for this change, isn't there, Mark?" Lisa asked in a low voice, looking up at him with somber eyes. "It's because of us. The talk going around about us."

Mark turned to look out the window, appearing to study the tall office building across the street. "There was bound to be some gossip, Lee," he said quietly. "Especially about a man who's barely been a widower for ten months. So what if all we've had were a few lunches, dinner occasionally. You know how such gossip is frowned upon here. So everyone will simply be told that Dan Nolan is being given a secretary familiar with the firm's policies and procedures."

Lisa's well-shaped mouth, a mouth that showed the promise of sensuality, now curved into a slow, bitter smile. "Do you think anyone will believe it?"

Mark turned to face her. "No," he replied honestly. "And I don't care. I enjoy your company, Lee. I want to go on seeing you, if you're agreeable."

Lisa rose swiftly and approached Mark until she stood close enough to him that he smelled the distinctive fragrance of her perfume. "I'm agreeable, Mr. Connors," she said demurely, her eyes dancing with laughter.

"Miss Winters, I suggest you leave before I find some additional duties for you," Mark said suddenly.

"Yes, sir," she murmured, taking her leave.

"Lisa." His voice followed her out of the office. "Dan Nolan will be here Monday, and we're giving him John Stanton's office."

"Don't worry, I'll make sure everything is taken care of," she answered. Her manner was now that of an efficient secretary. "Good night, Mark. I'll see you tomorrow evening."

Lisa's smile disappeared as she walked outside. Dan Nolan, of all people! She had never met the man, but she had seen his picture in the newspaper, accompanying articles written on a few of his cases. He was rapidly becoming a lawyer well-known for his caustic tongue and fiery delivery in the courtroom. She knew him to be in his early thirties, single, good-looking and known also for his conquests of the opposite sex. Beautiful women vied for the honor of being at his side at various social functions. He was the type of man Lisa preferred to stay far away from. Instead, it seemed, she would be working just about as close to him as she could get!

Half an hour later, Lisa parked her car in the carport of her apartment and absently looked out at the silhouette of a tall, snow-covered mountain, dark against the early evening sky. The mountain wasn't a true mountain made of earth, rocks and snow, but was a facsimile of the famous Swiss Matterhorn, a popular Disneyland ride. Lisa noted that it wouldn't be long before summer would be here and the nightly fireworks displays would begin, fireworks that could easily be seen from her kitchen window.

Locking her car, she headed for her apartment. She was soon opening the door to the small place she shared with her cousin. The two girls had grown up in the same town, Ventura. They were still best friends, and still close to their parents, who approved of their joint living arrangement.

"Well, I see you timed your arrival well; I've just finished making dinner," her cousin called out.

"It shouldn't have taken you very long, since all you did was throw everything into the crock pot this morning before you left for work," Lisa teased, shrugging off her tan blazer.

Debra Stevens, Lisa's cousin and roommate, walked out of the compact kitchen, wiping her hands on an apron covering her jeans. Her long, dark brown hair was held away from her face with a cotton scarf, and her green eyes twinkled merrily.

"Beef stew is cheap, kid." Debra grinned. "Especially if there are more vegetables in it than meat."

"Well, whatever it is, I'm starved. I had to work through my lunch hour *and* stay late. Do I have time to change before we eat?"

"Sure," Debra replied, walking back into the kitchen.

Lisa went into the large bedroom the two young women shared. She quickly shed her tan skirt and gold-and-brown-striped silk shirt, changing into jeans and a yellow T-shirt. Hanging up her skirt, her mind flashed back to the conversation she had had with Mark before she left the office. "Drat Dan Nolan," she muttered between clenched teeth.

Going back into the kitchen, Lisa found that Debra had the table already set, with the earthenware crock pot in the center. Lisa sniffed appreciatively, remembering the lunch she had missed. "Is tomorrow your Saturday to work?" she asked Debra, as she sat down.

"Unfortunately, yes," Debra sighed. "Though I feel as if I'm going to come down with a good case of fleas any day now." She was referring to her job as a veterinary assistant at a large animal hospital. "How was your day?"

"Fine, until the end." Lisa grimaced. "Now that Mr. Stanton has retired, they've brought in a new lawyer."

"Oh? Anyone gorgeous and available?"

"It's Dan Nolan."

"Dan Nolan!" Debra squealed. "*The* Dan Nolan? The one who is always seen with rich and beautiful women? He sure is sexy-looking."

"Be that as it may, I have to work for him," Lisa said glumly.

"I think that's great. I *am* surprised, though, because I read an article about him in the newspaper once, and it seemed to indicate that he didn't believe in working for large firms. How did Patterson and Marsh manage to tempt him?" Debra asked.

"Who knows?" Lisa shrugged her shoulders. "But Mark told me that I'll be working for Dan Nolan as of Monday. It was a collective decision made by the senior partners. They make it sound like a promotion for me, of course."

"Didn't I tell you something like this would happen?" Debra said, without a trace of smugness in her voice. Her enthusiasm was for her cousin. "Those men are still living in the days when it was considered unseemly for the boss to date his secretary. They don't have any reason to fire you, so they'll just get you out of

13

Mark's sight all day. Maybe they think this will be enough to break up your relationship."

"Mark and I are only friends," Lisa said defensively. "A few dinners and they all believe we're having an affair."

Debra leaned back in her chair, a mischievous grin on her face. "Poor Lisa. Considered a fallen woman and not even close to being tainted."

"Look who's talking," Lisa jeered back good-naturedly. "Miss 'no' of all time."

"And it's going to stay my favorite word, too, if the dates I've had lately are any indication."

Lisa had always enjoyed Mark's company because he expected nothing from her; he simply wanted her to be a pleasant companion during their evenings together. This Saturday evening was no exception, as he escorted her to a well-known restaurant.

"You're not happy over this change, are you?" Mark asked quietly, studying the brandy in his glass as they relaxed after dinner.

Lisa set her cup of Irish coffee down and looked across the table at him. "I dislike having to change because of idle gossip." She sighed heavily. "I value my privacy and I feel as if it's been invaded. They make our friendship seem dirty, somehow."

"What they really want to put a stop to is my mid-life crisis." He smiled. "It's not considered seemly, even in these enlightened times, for a man over forty to chase after a young and attractive woman barely over twenty. Contrary to popular belief, there's still a name for a man like that. Especially when that man is one of the senior partners in an old and established law firm."

"Mark, you're a widower in the prime of your life, not some dirty old man chasing after teenagers," Lisa protested. "I understand that you still miss Ann. She was a warm and loving woman. But I don't think she would have wanted you to spend the rest of your life grieving for her. She valued life too much for that."

"You seem to know what Ann would want for me better than I do," he said sadly.

Lisa leaned forward, covering his hand with hers. "Because I would hope that my husband wouldn't grieve if I were gone," she said gently. "I would want him to go on living."

Later that evening Mark left Lisa at her door after a light good-night kiss on the lips. When she entered the apartment she found Debra curled up on the carpet surrounded by books.

"Early night," Debra commented, taking her glasses off. "Was Mark afraid you'd turn into a pumpkin if he kept you out too late?"

"I can see you've had an exciting evening," Lisa said, preferring to ignore her roommate's dry sarcasm, as she collapsed into a nearby easy chair.

"I'm charting Pat's horoscope." Debra was referring to the man she had been dating off and on for the past few months.

"And?"

"Everything is in his favor—and in mine." Debra smiled confidently. "Everything I read about his sign is so true of him. His calm, easy attitude toward life, the rare flare-ups of temper, everything. In fact, he's so true to form it almost scares me." She replaced her glasses on her nose.

Lisa grinned, knowing her cousin's passion for keeping her life geared to the stars. "I suppose you've also already studied up on Mark and me?"

"Right after you accepted that first dinner invitation from him," Debra said without shame.

"What did you find out about us?"

"He's too methodical for you, Lee," Debra said candidly. "I have an idea that you only date him right now because he doesn't demand anything from you. You want someone who won't make a heavy-handed pass at you. But there's going to come a time when you want fireworks and violin music and Mark Connors won't be able to give them to you."

"This is all too ridiculous." Lisa stood up, painfully aware that Debra's words were all too true. None of Mark's caresses or kisses had ever excited her in the least. "Astrology just isn't logical. And I don't think I'd care to go through life checking every day to see what was going to happen in the future. I'd rather be surprised. Right now, though, I'm tired; I think I'll go to bed." She said this over her shoulder as she walked toward the bedroom.

"Just wait until you find someone special and you want to find out about him," Debra called after her. "Then you'll be ready to ask my advice. And I'm not too sure if I'll be willing to give it. But stay away from a Pisces in any case."

Lisa spent the remainder of the weekend in not looking forward to going back to work. When Monday finally arrived, she was determined to give the effect of the professional, efficient secretary at first glance. Her rust-colored skirt and jacket, with an earth-toned silk

16

shirt, gave the desired effect. Her heavy hair, pinned up into a French twist, finished the picture.

Lisa arrived at the office while all was still quiet. She quickly scanned her new boss's office, assuring herself that all was ready. In a short time she transferred her personal belongings to her new desk. Then she went into the small room where the coffee maker was kept and soon had coffee brewing. Minutes later she carried a cup back to her desk, sipping the hot liquid.

"Good morning, Lisa." She looked up on hearing the familiar voice.

"Mr. Connors," she said formally, linking her hands in front of her on the top of her new desk.

"Lisa, I'd like you to meet Dan Nolan." Even Mark's voice seemed oddly tense and formal.

Lisa's eyes were cool as they passed from Mark to the tall figure behind him. She had to admit that Dan Nolan was very good-looking indeed. Well over six feet, he had dark blond hair that would lighten naturally in the bright summer sun and blue eyes that would undoubtedly warm with passion, though they were cool with disinterest right now.

"Dan, this is Lisa Winters. She's thoroughly familiar with our procedures and policies. I'm sure you'll find her very helpful."

"Mr. Nolan." Lisa formally inclined her head, allowing herself only a thin, polite smile. "Welcome to Patterson and Marsh."

"Thank you, Miss Winters." His well-shaped mouth seemed to twist into an amused grin. Was he aware of how much she disliked him already? "Or would you prefer Ms.?"

17

"Whichever you feel most comfortable with, Mr. Nolan," she replied demurely. When she turned toward Mark her smile was warmer than usual. "I left some notes for Barbara, telling her where the most important files might be found if they're not in their usual places. I'm sure she'll be fine, but she can call me with any questions if she needs to."

"Well, uh . . . yes, thank you." Mark shifted his stance, uncomfortable under the younger man's steady gaze. "I'll see you later, Nolan."

The two of them were now alone, but Lisa's eyes refused to waver in the face of his cool blue stare. "I've checked your office and it seems to have everything you might need," she said politely. "Of course, if you do need anything else, please let me know and I'll take care of it at once."

"I take my coffee black," Dan announced, walking into his office and looking around, not missing one book or furnishing during his visual inspection. "Naturally, I expect you to open any mail not marked personal," he called out to her. "With any correspondence I dictate I prefer to see a typed rough draft first. And I assume that you're well versed in screening calls."

Lisa sat tensely at her desk, slowly counting to ten, then she began all over again. Still muttering under her breath, she rose and walked toward the coffee room. One of the secretaries passed her with a sly grin. "Lucky you," she whispered. "He's a doll."

"The kind I'd like to stick pins in," Lisa said through clenched teeth.

Moments later, carrying a filled coffee cup, black, she entered Dan's office. Suppressing the childish urge

18

to dump the hot coffee in his lap, she set the cup on his desk.

"Your coffee, Mr. Nolan," she said crisply.

"Thank you, Miss Winters." His husky voice held a trace of amusement. "If you had poured that hot coffee in my lap, you would have made, in addition to me, many lovely ladies very unhappy."

"Well, we couldn't have that, could we?" Lisa said tartly, turning to leave.

"Miss Winters." The deep voice stopped her in her tracks. "I don't want an office robot, so I would appreciate a secretary with a little courtesy and someone who will look out for her boss's interests and welfare. I hope I can count on you for that."

"I'm sure you won't have cause to find fault with any of my secretarial skills, Mr. Nolan." She refused to give him a direct answer. There was something unnerving in the way he was looking at her, as if he was trying to see into her soul. She would have to watch her step with this man.

"You may go, Miss Winters."

Lisa pointedly closed the door behind her as she returned to her desk. And she was still fuming later that morning as she surveyed the stack of papers sitting on her desk, waiting to be sorted and filed. Dan Nolan had wasted no time in going through the files, deciding what was to be kept and what was to be stored in the office archives.

"Smile and light up that pretty face." A familiar voice sounded in front of her.

"Oh, Mark. Aren't you supposed to be in court this morning? The Carstairs case?"

"That excellent memory is at work again, I see,"

Mark lightly teased, then his face sobered as he gazed down at her upturned face. "But the other side won a postponement. Have lunch with me?"

"I can't today," she sighed. "I have a new boss to break in, remember? And tons of filing to get out of the way."

"Just don't break him in too well." His face darkened.

"Jealous already, Mark?" Lisa asked lightly.

"Did you want to see me, Connors?" Dan Nolan's deep voice sounded from over Lisa's shoulder. Flushing, Lisa looked up at his enigmatic face.

"No, and I see nothing wrong in conversing with my former secretary," Mark said stiffly.

"These letters have to be ready for this afternoon's mail." Dan handed several handwritten sheets to Lisa, ignoring Mark.

"Yes, Mr. Nolan." Lisa kept her eyes downcast to hide the angry sparkle in them.

"I'll see you later, Lisa," Mark murmured, leaving her desk.

Nodding, she glanced through the sheets of bold handwriting, quickly scanning the contents. "At least he can spell," she thought to herself.

When Lisa left the office at the end of the day, her mood hadn't improved. And when she entered her apartment she closed the door behind her with more force than was strictly necessary.

"It looks like you need this more than I do." Debra handed Lisa a filled wine glass. "How was day one with Dan Nolan?"

"He had barely installed himself in the office before he was telling me how to do my job, how he takes his

20

coffee and even how to open the mail!" Lisa said with annoyance. "Dan Nolan is more machine than human. A computer has more emotions than he does."

"Computers have no emotions," Debra pointed out.

"I feel as if we're running a race to see who will crack first. I would barely finish one task and he would have another to be done. Right away, of course. How I would love to see him in Siberia." Her eyes glinted dangerously over the rim of her glass. "I bet if you cut him open you'd find wires and terminals inside instead of veins and muscles."

"This man sounds like he's going to be a real challenge for you. You're not going to be able to anticipate his every thought the way you did with Mark, either. He's playing a game with you, Lee. A game you may not win."

"Oh, yes, I will," Lisa said confidently. "Even machines have to slow down sometime, and I intend to be there when he does."

Lisa soon found out differently. Dan Nolan was tireless, throwing himself into his work and expecting the same from his secretary. Many evenings Lisa worked late, dragging herself home so exhausted that she wanted only a hot bath and bed.

"You're worn out," Debra scolded her one Saturday as they relaxed, drinking tall glasses of iced tea after finishing their housework. "You can't keep up this pace much longer without ending up sick."

"He'd only have the work delivered here." Lisa sighed. "Deb, he's in the office before I get there in the morning, and he's still working away when I leave. Even if he spends the day in court, he still comes back to the office afterward to check up on things. He does all but sleep there. And for all I know he may do that, too."

"That could really ruin a man's social life." Debra grinned.

"Not so long as he can see his women at lunchtime." She made a face. "So far, there have been Cheryl, Heather, Stacey and Rhonda. Plus someone named Morgan Grant who calls him just about every day. If she matches her sexy voice, when she comes into the office, there are going to be some heart attacks among the senior staff."

"Morgan, huh? As in Morgan Le Fay?"

"Probably." Lisa sighed, inspecting her nails, noting she was badly in need of a manicure. "I'm sure she'll show up some day. He seems to have scheduled them all, so he won't forget anyone."

"Are you and Mark going out tonight?" Debra asking, changing the subject.

"Yes, to dinner and a movie. I've had to turn him down so much these past few weeks that I hated to turn him down again, but I told him we would have to make it an early night."

That evening, Mark viewed the dark smudges under Lisa's eyes with concern. Then he said, "Some people are saying that the two of you have some kind of a private feud going on. It doesn't look good when that happens, Lee."

She closed her eyes in frustration. "Lately it seems I can't do anything right for anyone in that firm," she said angrily. "I'm too nice to one boss and not nice enough to another. If I have such trouble pleasing people, why do they bother keeping me on? I don't like the man, Mark. And not only because he's so chauvinistic. He's so egotistical you'd think the firm would fall apart without him. His sense of self-importance is galling. Heaven only knows how he thinks we got on before he showed up."

Mark sighed, then he chose his words carefully. "What I'm about to tell you, Lee, is in strict confidence. I'm sure you don't need me to tell you that our office activity has slowed down a great deal in the past few years. I myself haven't had a new case in two months, and my caseload isn't all that heavy."

"Are you trying to say we're going broke, Mark?" she asked in a low voice.

"No, but we are losing a great deal of money right now. And Dan Nolan has the contacts we need to pull ourselves up," he told her. "No matter what you think about his personality, he is an excellent lawyer."

"He also had his own practice before, didn't he? Why did he decide to join a firm all of a sudden?"

"I don't know. But we're certainly not going to look a gift horse in the mouth."

"Shouldn't we go so we won't miss the movie?" Lisa murmured, feeling suddenly uneasy at Mark's serious tone.

"Um, you're right." Mark glanced down at his watch, distracted now from the topic of Dan Nolan and the firm's future.

Lisa was glad that the movie they had chosen to see was a comedy that didn't require much concentration because the gravity of Mark's statements kept running through her mind. She had to admit to herself that Dan Nolan *was* an excellent lawyer. After typing his briefs during the past few weeks she could see what a fighter he was for his clients. And he definitely preferred a case that required a struggle, rather than one that was all smiles and bows.

Lisa was still quiet during the drive back to her apartment. When Mark stopped his car in front of the building, he half turned in his seat to face her. "You've been a pretty quiet girl this evening," he remarked, his finger idly playing with a stray curl lying on her shoulder.

"I guess it's because I feel so relaxed." She turned to smile at him.

Mark's eyes darkened as they gazed into Lisa's eyes, the color of jade green now. His hand on her shoulder tightened as his head bent toward her for a gentle kiss. "Lee," he breathed, resting his lips against hers.

Lisa closed her eyes, allowing herself to relax and enjoy Mark's kiss. But just as Debra had predicted, there were no fireworks. She could have wept with frustration when Mark lifted his head. She was half-puzzled and half-angry that the expression on Mark's face told her that he hadn't even noticed her lack of reponse.

"Do you know how beautiful you are?" he asked huskily. "There were times in the office when I had trouble concentrating on my dictation because I preferred to look at you. I never realized how important you were to me until I lost you as my secretary. How much more important you were to me than just a secretary. You mean more than that, Lee."

"Oh, Mark." Lisa laid her palm against his cheek. Now she felt even more confused. "There are much prettier girls than me in the office."

"I've never noticed," he muttered, claiming her lips again.

Lisa's arms crept up around Mark's neck, and she willed herself to respond to his kiss. She reminded herself that his wife had been dead for less than a year. After a love-filled, happy marriage that had lasted over fifteen years, this was still all new to him. But still his kisses didn't affect her at all. Maybe she was expecting too much. Perhaps those fireworks only happened in books. A fire in the blood, a singing in the veins, a call from one body to another.

"I guess I should let you go in," Mark said, reluctantly releasing her from his embrace. "I'll walk you to the door."

At her door he pressed one last hard kiss against her lips. "I'll see you on Monday," he said. "And, Lisa, please remember, no matter what you think of Nolan as a person, he *is* a fine lawyer."

"Then he should stay in the courtroom more and in my hair less," Lisa retorted.

"Ah, but it's such lovely hair," Mark said, laughing softly. "But I guess I shouldn't say too much in his favor. He's a very good-looking man and more the age for you. Half the women in the office would give their eyeteeth to have him even look at them."

"Don't worry, I'm definitely *not* in that half. Dan Nolan is far from being my type. Good night, Mark." She smiled up at him.

Debra was already in bed, reading, when Lisa entered the bedroom. "I see he got you in early, true to your word," Debra commented dryly. "Or is it past Mark's bedtime?"

"He's only forty-four, not in dotage," Lisa argued, quickly shedding her clothes and slipping on a nightgown. "You're making him sound as if he's ready for a wheelchair and a warm fire!"

"Oh, Lee!" Debra said, exasperated. "Don't settle for lukewarm kisses and half-hearted embraces. Go out and find yourself a man with some warm blood in his veins. Someone like Dan Nolan. I bet he could set off a lot of fireworks in a woman's body."

"Dan Nolan! Dan Nolan!" Lisa shouted. "I am so tired of hearing that name. Why can't the man be mentioned less so I can enjoy my weekend in peace? I happen to be very happy with Mark, so I would appreciate it if you would just leave the matter alone." She crawled into bed, pulling the covers over her head.

"I'm sorry, Lee," Debra said softly. "I don't want to make you angry. I just don't want to see you unhappy with the wrong man. Please believe that I'm only looking out for you."

"Then please let me do things my way," Lisa replied in a weary voice. "Good night, Deb."

Not long after Debra turned the light out, but Lisa didn't find sleep easy to achieve. And when it did come, ironically, she dreamed about the very man she had so resolutely determined not to have anything to do with.

Chapter Two

Lisa refilled her coffee cup for the third time that morning, feeling as if she were drowning in coffee.

"You know where all that caffeine will get you, don't you?" Barbara, Mark's new secretary, pointed out as she poured coffee for herself.

"Mr. Nolan has been on the ceiling since he came in this morning," Lisa said tautly, liberally adding cream to her cup. "There's no way I could manage to join him there."

"Since you don't care to join me on the ceiling, Miss Winters, perhaps you wouldn't mind joining me in my office for some dictation." Dan Nolan's mocking voice sounded from over her shoulder.

Barbara melted away with a murmured excuse.

"I'll be there directly, Mr. Nolan," Lisa said coolly, her outer composure totally unruffled, a complete contradiction to her inner turmoil. How could this man throw her whole being out of kilter, keeping her from being her usual calm self? And all with only a word or a glance from those unnerving blue eyes.

Lisa made sure to take her time walking back to her desk. Picking up a steno pad and pencils, she walked into the inner office and seated herself across from Dan Nolan. He was sitting behind his desk, glancing through several typewritten sheets.

"To Mr. William Stanley," he began crisply, barely pausing for breath as he dictated several letters to Lisa. Her pencil flew over the paper drawing its own special symbols. "No need for rough drafts this time," he said. "I'll sign these after lunch." His tone indicated a curt dismissal, though he didn't look up.

"Yes, sir." Lisa gracefully rose to leave.

"Miss Winters."

Lisa halted her retreat and turned. "Yes, Mr. Nolan?" Her voice was polite, nothing more.

"Is it possible for us to be friends?" The expression in his blue eyes was unreadable.

Lisa was taken aback by his question. "Do you mean a truce?"

"Whatever will work for us." His voice was steady, so were his eyes, as he studied the conflicting expression crossing her face.

Lisa was aware that her pulse was speeding up under his unwavering gaze. It was almost as if he had physically touched her, but she didn't even like the man!

28

"I'll be sure that my distemper shots are brought up to date then, Mr. Nolan," she said demurely.

Amusement flickered in the depths of Dan Nolan's blue eyes. "Would you please make lunch reservations for two at twelve-thirty at that new French restaurant?" He now reverted back to his old self.

Lisa returned to her desk, unaware of a smile playing about her lips. She had just finished typing up her dictation when the phone rang.

"Lisa, a Miss Grant is here to see Mr. Nolan," the receptionist in the front lobby informed her.

"Thank you, Tina. I'll be right out."

A puzzled frown crossed her brow, as Lisa quickly flipped through the pages of the appointment calendar. Finally, feeling defeated, she pushed the intercom line and waited for an answer.

"Yes?"

"Mr. Nolan, a Miss Grant is here to see you, but I can't seem to find her name in the appointment book."

"Possibly because Miss Grant is here to meet me for lunch," he replied with forced patience. "Would you bring her back here, please?"

Lisa walked out to the lobby and easily spotted the woman. "Miss Grant?" Her face was a polite mask. "I'm Miss Winters, Mr. Nolan's secretary. He asked that I show you to his office. I'm afraid he's running a bit behind schedule this morning."

The tall, well-groomed woman looked Lisa over with indifference. And when she said thank you, Lisa knew it was definitely the same voice she had heard over the telephone so many times before.

Lisa guessed that the woman was in her late twenties

and not the type to wear anything that didn't bear a well-known designer's label. Her blonde hair was smoothed back in a chignon, revealing cold, porcelain features. Her raw-silk suit of deep rose and her high heels, with narrow straps at the ankles, made Lisa feel like a gauche schoolgirl. I bet she had a nose job, Lisa thought cattily, as she knocked on her boss's door, then opened it to allow the other woman to pass through.

"Surprise, darling, I'm on time." Morgan Grant's voice was a throaty purr as she brushed past Lisa and closed the door.

A few moments later, when the door opened and the two walked out, Lisa noted how well-matched they were. Morgan Grant, with her cold patrician features, and Dan Nolan, with his rugged good looks.

"Have a good lunch, Mr. Nolan," Lisa murmured politely.

"We will, Miss Winters, we will." Lisa could have sworn to amusement in his husky voice.

"We'll knock off work early on Friday for Sue's baby shower," Barbara told Lisa that day over lunch. "Mr. Marsh is going to call her into his office for dictation around three-thirty to give us time to set everything out. He's even going to buy champagne for the shower."

"Probably to cry in," Lisa said wryly. "He's been letting everyone know he's sick to death about losing her. Sue has that man eating out of her hand."

"Not like some people I know," Barbara murmured.

"Has Mark been giving you a bad time?" Lisa asked in surprise. "He's always been so understanding that it's hard to imagine that he might be temperamental to work for."

"You know very well who I'm talking about. People are talking about the feud between *you* and *your* boss."

"We are *not* feuding," Lisa retorted.

"Well, that's the way everyone else sees it," Barbara told her. "Look, Lee, you have to expect talk. Unfortunately in our office there are some people who don't have time for anything else but. Plus, Dan Nolan is very good-looking and single and you're definitely not ugly. Some people wonder if he made a pass at you and you turned him down. Of course, I can't see that happening." Her smile told Lisa what *her* answer would have been had it been she.

"None of that is true." Lisa leaned forward in her chair. "He's just too high and mighty for my taste, that's all. I'm not going to fall all over him and I intend for him to know that. And we get along fine. There is no feud and no hot and heavy love affair. So would you please let that get around to discourage any nasty rumors?"

"I'll do what I can," Barbara promised.

On Tuesday afternoon, Lisa was grateful to leave the office on time, since Dan had spent the afternoon in court. She let herself into the apartment and headed for the bathroom, desiring only a nice, relaxing hot bath. When she was in the midst of towel-drying her freshly washed hair she heard the sound of the front door.

"Hi," she greeted Debra as she walked out of the bathroom.

"Great! Am I glad you came home on time tonight," Debra said with an air of mysterious excitement.

"Mr. Nolan was in court all afternoon so I was glad to get out of there on time."

"I met a fascinating woman this afternoon, a psychic. She's agreed to give us readings this evening. Oh, Lisa," Debra continued, "I have a feeling that this could prove very interesting for you. I'll even treat you to dinner first."

Lisa sighed, feeling as if she would be fighting a losing battle if she tried to resist. "What exactly do you wear to one of these things?" she asked, resigned to her fate.

"Anything. Just let me take a quick shower and we'll go." Debra hurried past Lisa, afraid her cousin might change her mind.

After a quick dinner at a local restaurant, Debra drove to a small, nearby beach community, steering her small Triumph through the narrow, winding streets. As each street grew darker and narrower, Lisa felt uneasy.

"Her name is Xenia," Debra told her as she parked the car in front of a small house with a gaily painted green door.

"Xenia?" Lisa was ready to turn back, but her cousin kept a firm grip on her arm as they approached the door. She was unprepared to see a smiling white-haired lady in her late sixties answer the door.

"Hello, Debra. And you must be Lisa," she greeted them warmly. "Please come in."

Lisa entered hesitantly, looking around the tiny living room. A round table stood in one corner, a large crystal ball in its center.

"Who wants to be first?" Xenia asked.

"I will," Lisa volunteered, anxious to get it over with.

The older woman indicated where they should sit. First she asked Lisa her birthday and time of birth and wrote down the information.

"An Aries." Xenia smiled. "Impulsive, aggressive, but your personality tends to hold you back. You try to do too many things at once, don't you? You lead with your emotions, not with your head."

She handed Lisa a deck of cards, instructing her to shuffle them before she laid them one by one on a cloth marked with squares, whose outlines she was to follow.

"There's a man in your life now who expects something from you," Xenia told Lisa. "More, perhaps, than you know. He's quite a bit older than you are, and he is inflexible. Does that someone sound familiar to you?"

Stunned, Lisa could only nod. For the next hour she became even more surprised as the woman talked accurately about her work and friends. Xenia smiled when she reached a particular card. "Your love card." She tapped the pasteboard with a forefinger. "This man I like. He seems like a lot of fun, sincere, down-to-earth. He'll seem uncaring, but it isn't true. He's a man of action, but only when he's ready. Hold on to him. He's good for you. Be cautious of jealousy and harsh words, though, or you will lose him. Oh, and you may not think so, but his eyes are on you a great deal."

Lisa's mind whirled with this revelation. She knew Mark had to be the first man Xenia mentioned. But who could the second man be? Had she even met him yet?

When the two cousins traded places, Lisa used

shorthand to take down every word of Debra's prediction, as Xenia spoke of her work and the man in her future. Lisa wondered if people specifically came to someone like Xenia to find out their romantic future. Personally, she preferred to find out on her own, in due time.

"Hm, I wonder who the two men in your life are," Debra mused, shooting Lisa a sly glance as they drove home. "One sounds like Mark. Think number two could be Dan Nolan?"

"I should hope not," Lisa said sharply. "He already has a harem to fill his lunch hours. I don't intend to become a groupie at this late date.

"I have to meet this man. You haven't been the same since you began working for him."

"What do you mean?" Lisa demanded.

"Let's just say that you take much more time with your appearance than you did when you were working for Mark," Debra said smugly. "Need I say more?"

"I don't want to talk about it," Lisa replied tightly, staring straight ahead.

Debra hid a smile as she shifted gears and turned down the street to their apartment house.

Lisa searched frantically through the file drawers, muttering under her breath.

"What on earth are you doing?" demanded a deep male voice from behind.

"Trying to find the file on the Stuart case," she replied clenching her teeth.

"Do you mean to say the ever-efficient Miss Winters has misfiled something?" Dan Nolan perched himself on the edge of Lisa's desk and flashed her a mocking smile.

"It *isn't* misfiled!" she snapped. "I'm just afraid it may have gotten stuck inside another folder, that's all."

"Did you happen to look on my desk?" he asked reasonably.

Lisa sighed an angry breath. "There was no reason for me to look on your desk."

"There is if I was looking through that file this morning and didn't get a chance to put it back," he said evenly. Then his attention was caught by several type-written sheets lying on Lisa's desk. He reached down and picked them up, then began to read.

"I typed those on my own time," Lisa said hastily, recognizing the sheets as the notes she had taken for Debra the previous evening.

"You believe in this stuff?"

"My roommate conned me into going with her to a psychic. Since she can't read shorthand I typed them up during my lunch hour."

"Don't be so defensive," Dan chided. "It doesn't matter to me when you typed them up. You've put in a lot of overtime the past few weeks." He straightened up. "I'll be working late again tonight, but there's no need for you to stay. Why don't you even leave early, say around three?"

Lisa looked up with surprise. She hadn't realized he had appreciated the evenings when she had stayed late to catch up on the heavy workload.

"Does that surprise you, Miss Winters? I can be human after all." His voice mocked her as he walked into his office. "Oh, Miss Winters, don't forget the Stuart file."

35

For the balance of the week Lisa was continually surprised by Dan Nolan's insight into her activities. Although he still expected a great deal from her, he didn't overload her with work. Friday morning, Lisa realized she hadn't told him about the surprise baby shower planned for that afternoon. She waited until he had settled himself behind his desk before walking into the office.

"Mr. Nolan, we've planned a baby shower for Sue, Mr. Marsh's secretary, this afternoon, at about four," she began hesitantly. "If it's all right with you, Tina has offered to screen all your incoming calls."

"What's wrong, Miss Winters?" he taunted. "Afraid I'll order you to stay at your desk until five? As a matter of fact, even we stodgy old lawyers were invited, too."

Lisa hid a smile. Dan Nolan was anything but stodgy. Seated behind his desk, his suit jacket discarded and his shirt sleeves rolled up to his elbows, he was all male. And one not easily forgotten.

Sue, the young, dark-haired secretary, was duly surprised when she walked into the conference room later that afternoon to a champagne party in her honor. Under the influence of the champagne, Lisa's cheeks were soon becomingly flushed and her green eyes sparkled brightly.

"Tell me, Miss Winters, after another glass or two of champagne, would you allow me to take you home with me and have my way with you?" A man's husky voice, teasing, sounded near her.

Startled, Lisa turned around to see Dan Nolan's smiling face. She could feel her blood racing as she gazed, mesmerized, at his sturdy features. What really surprised her was that she suddenly realized she would willingly have gone anywhere with him if he had seriously suggested it.

"I . . . I don't really enjoy drinking." She hoped her voice sounded steadier than she felt.

"What a shame," Dan murmured before moving away.

Lisa set her glass down, afraid her trembling hand would soon drop it.

"How about dinner with an ardent admirer?" Mark's voice was low as he stood next to her.

Lisa looked across the room and saw Morgan Grant standing in the doorway. A moment later Dan was by her side, flashing her a warm smile. Lisa suddenly felt curiously flat. "That sounds like a lovely idea, Mark," she said distractedly. "Let me get my purse."

During dinner Mark studied Lisa's face. "You've changed Lee," he told her.

"For the better, I hope," she said lightly as she sipped her wine.

"It's hard to say." His eyes narrowed in thought. "You seem to have grown quieter, no longer as bubbly and outgoing as you used to be. More serious."

"There was a time when you thought I was *too* bubbly and outgoing," Lisa pointed out.

"Only when you acted like a child, forgetting you were an adult," Mark said stiffly.

Lisa's temper began rising at his words. Who was he to tell her how she behaved? "Perhaps it would be a good idea, then, if we called it an evening," she said tautly.

Mark sighed, realizing he had gone too far. Lisa stayed coolly silent during the drive back to the office parking lot, where her car was parked.

"Lee, I'm sorry," Mark finally said as he stopped his car alongside hers. "I didn't mean to make you angry."

"I'm not angry, Mark," she said quietly.

"Then why are you acting so childish now?" The moment the words were out, he regretted them. "Wait, Lee, that's not what I meant."

"Good night, Mark." Lisa got out of his car and stiffly walked toward her own. She ignored his call for her return and got into her car, revving the engine more than necessary. Tires squealing on the pavement, she raced out of the parking lot.

There were tears in her eyes, but she knew they had nothing to do with Mark.

Arriving home, she was glad to have the apartment to herself, as Debra was out for the evening. Lisa flopped down in an easy chair, closing her eyes, feeling suddenly very weary. A picture of Dan Nolan with Morgan Grant flashed through her mind, and she wrinkled her nose in distaste. Lisa covered her face with her hands, wanting to scream with frustration. Couldn't she ever get away from that man?

When Lisa arrived at work Monday morning, she was surprised to find a small stack of handwritten sheets on her desk with a list of instructions attached, evidence that her boss had been working over the weekend. Sighing, she uncovered her typewriter to begin her work.

"Good morning, Lisa, and how was your weekend?" she asked herself, as she put paper into the typewriter. "It was very nice, thank you," she mocked herself as she replied.

"Was it?"

With a burning face, Lisa looked up to find her boss's eyes fixed on her with amusement.

"It's bad enough when you talk to yourself, Miss Winters," Dan Nolan said, as he walked into his office. "But answering yourself could get you committed."

"That only started the day I began working for you," she couldn't help answering.

"Good. I was afraid you were sick. Glad to hear you're back to your old sweet self," he rejoined, this time closing his office door behind him and leaving for court.

Lisa bent over her typewriter again, glad that Dan Nolan was going to be out of the office all day. Their truce certainly hadn't done them much good for long, or had it? It only seemed to work when she was at her desk and he was in court.

The accuracy of that thought occurred to her later that day as she walked to her car. He had called in once, during a recess in the trial, for some information, and they had managed to be perfectly pleasant to each other. So why was it so impossible for them to be nice to each other in person?

Her car was slow to start, but she hardly noticed because she was so busy pondering Dan Nolan and the strange effect he had on her.

But she had nothing on her mind but her car Friday morning, when she stood beside it in the apartment parking lot, a service station tow truck beside her.

"But I can't have a dead battery!" Lisa wailed.

"Your car has to be put on a battery charger for at least eight hours," the young mechanic told her. "I could jump-start it for you now, but it wouldn't last."

"All right, whatever." She sighed. "Do whatever needs to be done."

Lisa went back to her apartment and called the office to inform them she'd be late coming in. She was glad that her boss wasn't due in until eleven, which she thought as she explained her problem to Tina, saying she would be in as soon as possible. As it happened, it was past ten before a frustrated Lisa entered the office.

"You picked a fine day to be late, Miss Winters," Dan Nolan snapped, walking out of his office carrying a sheaf of papers. "Didn't you think to let someone know?"

"I did," she snapped back. "Tina was supposed to leave a note for you on your desk. Besides, you weren't due in until eleven, and I knew I'd be here by then."

"So, since I wasn't due in until later, you decided you could do likewise?" Dan's eyes were dark with anger.

"Rest assured that it won't happen again," Lisa said coldly. She pointedly studied the papers on her desk, until she heard his door close abruptly. Her angry expression changed to one of dismay, as she realized that he had made a great many changes in a lengthy brief she had been typing on and off all week. She had thought she was finished with that project and now it was an incomplete typing job that would easily take her more than half a day to complete, barring interruptions. Silently heaping curses on her boss's head, she got out paper and began working.

Lisa became even more vexed as the day wore on. There was no time for her to take even a short lunch break. And it seemed that every time she turned around the phone rang again, bringing her more problems to deal with. It was late afternoon when she finally finished the typing and carried the papers back into the inner office. Dan Nolan didn't even look up as she set the stack of papers down in front of him. Gritting her teeth, she walked back to her desk.

Half an hour later, while Lisa was busy catching up on her filing, Dan walked out of his office, a dark look on his face.

"It still doesn't work as it's typed," he said flatly, tossing the papers back on her desk. "These additional new changes are going to have to be incorporated into the brief, and I'll need it by tonight."

"Tonight!" Lisa wailed in dismay. "But it's Friday."

"I don't care what day it is, Miss Winters. I'm sure that, with your excellent skills, you can get this done in no time."

Lisa swallowed the bitter words that rose in her throat. Sitting down at the typewriter, she glanced through the pages and saw that Dan had made added notations in bold handwriting on each page. Sighing, she inserted a fresh piece of paper into the typewriter and began typing.

"I should know this all by heart by now," she grumbled, her fingers flying over the typewriter keys.

By the time she finished retyping the lengthy brief, her back was aching from sitting so long in one position. Glancing at the clock she was not surprised to find it was past seven o'clock. Ripping the paper out of the typewriter, she quickly scanned the sheet for errors before adding it to the small stack on her desk. Lisa then walked over to the copy machine to run off a copy for her files. "So help me, if he wants this typed again I'll tell him to type it himself," she complained to herself as she punched the button on the copy machine.

Dan Nolan's office was dark, except for the lamp burning on his desk, when Lisa walked in. She felt a moment's compassion for him as she noted the visible signs of strain on his face, then she quickly squelched the feeling. "Finished," she said stiffly, laying the sheets in front of him.

He looked up, tiredly rubbing his hand over his face before he began leafing through the pages, concentrating on the paragraphs he had made the changes in. "Very good. Thank you."

"If that's all, then I'll leave now." Lisa's voice was cool and distant as she turned to leave the office.

"Tell me something personal, Miss Winters, if you don't mind. Why do you persist in dating Mark Connors when you must know very well that he'll never marry you?" her boss asked suddenly.

Startled by his question, Lisa could only turn to stare at him with angry eyes. "I don't believe that's any of your business," she said coldly.

Dan's face creased in a crooked grin. "Hit a sore spot, did I? He'll always put the firm first and his women second. Besides, his archaic mind would never accept marriage to a mere secretary. An affair with her, yes. Marriage, no."

"Why, Mr. Nolan, I had no idea you had such strong feelings about morals and marriage," Lisa said sarcastically. "Your concern for my welfare is overwhelming."

"It's hard to believe that you obviously enjoy being the bridesmaid and not the bride," he said cruelly.

Lisa clenched her fists, feeling the tensions of the day build up to a raging tide. "My private life is none of your business."

"Do you plan on becoming Connors' mistress?" Dan

persisted, his eyes narrowed in speculation. "Or, are you already?"

"Why don't you just worry about your own love life?" Lisa refused to let her threatening tears fall. "You should concentrate more on Morgan Grant. I'm sure she'd appreciate it." She turned, all but stumbling. But she had barely taken three steps when two strong hands gripped her shoulders and spun her around.

"You're crying," Dan said with quiet astonishment.

"No, I'm not." She resisted the urge to sniff loudly.

His forefinger tenderly touched her damp cheek. "I didn't intend to make you cry, Lisa," he said gently, using her first name as easily as if he had always used it. "I just don't want to see you hurt. Connors isn't worth it."

"Why don't you just leave me alone?" she begged.

"Where's the growling Miss Winters I know?" Dan coaxed with a soft chuckle. Looking down at her tear-stained face, his eyes darkened and his head lowered. Seeing his intent, Lisa struggled in his grasp.

"No!" she protested, as Dan's mouth descended firmly to hers.

Dan's arms tightened, pulling Lisa against his hard body. His mouth moved over hers, causing tingling sensations to run up and down her spine. Then it moved upward, as his tongue licked the salty dampness from her cheeks. As if under a spell, Lisa moved her face, now wanting Dan's lips on hers. A low laugh of triumph sounded in his throat as he claimed her lips again. Her arms crept up around his neck, and she let her fingers tangle in his thick hair. Lisa's body felt alive under his caresses. She hadn't dreamed that a man's touch could cause her pulse to race so madly.

"I don't know what I'm going to do with you yet," Dan murmured cryptically. "But then, how can I, when I don't even know what I'm going to do with myself?" Groaning, he pushed her away with evident reluctance. "Come on, I'm taking you to dinner and then home, before I get any more ideas."

"What makes you think I need to be taken home?" Lisa asked breathlessly.

Dan's lazy grin appeared, melting her insides. "I happened to pick up the phone when the garage called about your car, a fact that you didn't bother to mention to me this morning. And since I happen to know that the garage closed over an hour ago, it stands to reason that you need a ride home. So go get your things."

Lisa was still in a daze as she took her purse out of her desk, while Dan turned off his desk lamp and picked up his suit jacket and briefcase. In the confines of the elevator, Lisa's senses were keenly aware of the tall man standing beside her.

They were silent as they walked out into the dimly lit parking lot. Dan led her toward a tan Buick, holding the door for her before walking around to the driver's side. Sliding behind the wheel, he flipped on the ignition.

"Since it's Friday night I doubt we'll be able to get a table right away, no matter where we go. So I hope you're not in any hurry," he commented.

"No hurry."

Dan drove toward the outskirts of town, choosing a restaurant reminiscent of an old country inn. After giving his name to the headwaiter, he steered Lisa into the bar.

Throughout their meal, Dan quizzed Lisa endlessly

about herself, yet imparted scant information about his own life.

"Wait a minute," she finally protested, laughing. "I'm beginning to feel as if I'm on the witness stand. Is this how you're able to win so many cases?"

"The mark of a good lawyer." Dan leaned back in his chair, studying her closely. "You have beautiful eyes. Liquid emeralds."

Lisa turned her head away to hide the warmth stealing into her cheeks.

"Let's get out of here," Dan then said, signaling the waiter for their check.

The ride to Lisa's apartment was silent once she had given Dan the address and directions. She still felt puzzled at glimpsing this new side of her boss—a less arrogant side, but just as frightening. All too soon, his car pulled up in front of her apartment house.

"Thank you for dinner and for the ride home." Lisa turned to him with a smile, fumbling for the door handle. "Don't worry about seeing me in."

"I always see my ladies to the door," Dan informed her crisply.

At the apartment, Lisa fumbled with her key until Dan took it out of her hand and inserted it into the lock. Before she could open the door, he pulled her back into his arms. "If you pack a picnic lunch tomorrow, I'll bring the wine." His warm breath fanned her cheek as he spoke.

"Is that a request or an order?" Lisa asked.

"I'll make it an order. Then I know you'll do it." He was unabashed. "You always follow my orders."

"So far," she teased.

"Be ready at nine." Dan pressed a hard kiss against

her lips. "I better go before I change my mind and carry you off right now."

"Would that be so bad?" Lisa asked provocatively.

Dan gazed down at her face, his expression unfathomable as he studied the emerald depths of her eyes. "I'll see you in the morning." He reached behind her and opened the door before gently pushing her inside.

Later, lying in bed, Lisa recalled the feeling of Dan's lips on hers and the now familiar warmth spread through her body again, making her restless. It was some time before she was able to fall asleep.

Chapter Three

The following morning Lisa was up early, dressing quickly in jeans and a T-shirt. She walked over to the garage to pick up her car, and when she got back to the apartment Debra was already in the kitchen, drinking a cup of coffee and reading a magazine. She looked up in surprise, since Lisa was not usually one to get going first thing on a Saturday morning.

"To what do we owe the honor?" Debra asked brightly. "Unless it has something to do with your late night last evening."

"Dan is picking me up at nine, and we're going on a picnic," Lisa said casually, as she picked up a mug and poured herself some coffee.

"Dan? Do you mean *the* Dan Nolan who you constantly curse for making your working life so miserable?"

"I never said he made it miserable," Lisa said carefully. "Just that he was too arrogant for my taste."

"And that's why you're going out with him today, I suppose," Debra said archly. "Because you can't stand him. What brought about this sudden change?"

"We just decided to have a truce," Lisa said, avoiding her cousin's gaze. "That's all. For more amiable working conditions."

"Hm, and I just bet you did more than shake hands on it, too," Debra said mischievously, noting the flush on Lisa's face. "Aha, I was right! He kissed you good night, didn't he?"

"He isn't the first man to kiss me," Lisa protested. "And I doubt he'll be the last."

Ignoring Debra's grin, Lisa concentrated on getting the food ready and packing the picnic basket. She had just finished when the doorbell rang.

"I'll get it." Debra ran for the front door before Lisa could voice a protest. Opening the door, she looked their visitor over from head to toe. "You don't look so dangerous to me," she said glibly, much to Lisa's embarrassment. "Of course, appearances can be deceiving."

"True enough." Dan smiled.

"It sounds like he can be nasty, too," Debra said, turning to Lisa. "You better be careful; he may not have had his distemper shots yet."

"Deb . . ." Lisa's voice held a warning.

"Don't worry, I'm going." Debra looked up with a

mock-serious expression on her face as she gazed at Dan. "She's fragile, Mr. Nolan. Handle her with care."

"I intend to," he replied gravely, adding to the sport.

Dan turned to Lisa after the bedroom door closed behind Debra. He eyed her jeans and T-shirt with amusement. "Well, well, Miss Prim and Proper," he murmured. "I feel as if I'm seeing you out of uniform."

"The same holds with you," she said smiling, noting the well-worn jeans and faded T-shirt that hugged his lean frame. "I have everything ready to go."

"Fine." Dan picked up the basket, but before they left, he stopped her for a fleeting kiss on the lips.

"What was that for?" Lisa asked, startled.

"To see if last night had been a dream," Dan said seriously, then grinned. "Come on, wench, let's go."

It was some distance to Mason Park, in Irvine, but worth the drive. The green grass was lush underfoot, and there were plenty of trees to provide shade. Dan produced a Frisbee, and the two of them were soon spinning the bright yellow disc back and forth.

"You're not playing fair!" Lisa protested laughingly, after awhile. "You're much taller than I am so you can throw it higher. There's no way I can catch it."

"It's not my fault you're such a shrimp," he informed her, keeping a straight face.

"Oh, you!" Lisa aimed the Frisbee at Dan's midriff, shouting gleefully when she hit her target.

"Oh, so you want to play rough now, do you?" Dan growled, lunging at her.

Lisa laughed as she nimbly eluded Dan, but he finally managed a tackle by grabbing her at the knees, bringing her down in an ungraceful heap.

"Ow!" She winced at the sudden contact with the hard earth. "I wouldn't have done that to you."

"I would have let you," he said huskily, his eyes darkening as he gazed down at her.

"Sure of yourself, aren't you?" Lisa traced the outline of his lips with her forefinger, and he gently nibbled the tip. "Arrogant."

"Guilty." Dan's mouth moved along her jawline.

"Stubborn." Lisa found it difficult to breathe under Dan's sensual caresses.

"As a mule." His breath was warm against her face.

"Spoiled," she breathed.

"Rotten," Dan muttered.

"Childish."

"A regular baby." His tongue traced the outline of her ear, sending shivering sensations along her spine.

"Demanding." Lisa felt a warm mist surrounding her.

"Oh, yes." Dan tugged gently at her earlobe with his teeth, shifting his weight until she lay underneath him.

"Autocratic," Lisa whispered. Her mind refused to function. She moved restively under him.

"Stop it," he muttered thickly. His hand strayed beneath her T-shirt, caressing her softly rounded breasts.

"Dan," Lisa moaned softly.

"Say it again," he hoarsely ordered.

"What?"

"My name."

As Lisa's mouth formed his name, he covered her lips with his own. His kisses were long and drugging; she was drunk from his touch. Her hands slid under his shirt, her fingers fanning out over his hard, muscled chest. Abruptly, Dan broke the embrace, jackknifed away from her and sat up, shoving his fingers through his hair in an agitated gesture. His ragged breathing was the only sign of his heightened emotions.

"Dan," Lisa whispered, confused by his sudden withdrawal, as she reached out to stroke his back.

"Careful, my sweet," he chuckled, stilling her action with his hand. "You're very soft and warm in my arms. Also very responsive." She flushed at his words. "I suggest we eat before we decide to turn this lovely meadow into a bedroom."

Suddenly ashamed of her wanton response to Dan's lovemaking, Lisa stumbled to her feet and walked shakily over to the picnic hamper. She knelt down, unpacked the contents and set them out on the large cotton tablecloth with wooden motions.

"Lisa." Dan knelt down in front of her and cupped her face in his hands, lifting it up to him. "I don't want to use or hurt you. If I hurt you, I hurt myself."

"I—I've never responded to anyone the way I just did to you," she whispered jerkily, keeping her lashes lowered.

"Then I think it might be a good idea if you feed me, before I decide to have you as the main course instead," he teased.

A ghost of a smile touched Lisa's lips. Dan released her and sat back, getting out the bottle of wine and opening it. She soon relaxed, listening to his matter-of-fact compliments about the food.

"Um, you are a good cook," Dan said, munching on a chicken leg. "She can type, take dictation, and cook. What else can she do?"

"Sew," she replied, echoing his matter-of-fact manner. "And, in a pinch, I can change the oil in my car or a tire."

"That's dangerous. You could break a nail," Dan murmured, catching hold of Lisa's hand and bringing her fingers to his lips.

Lisa's breath caught in her throat at the sensual touch.

When the empty containers had been repacked in the hamper, Dan sat back against a tree, pulled Lisa down beside him and cradled her in his arms. "Just lie quiet." His murmur was husky in her ear.

Lisa laid her head against his cheek and closed her eyes. The wine from lunch, combined with the warmth of the day, left her drowsy, and the even rise and fall of his chest under her cheek made for a comforting rhythm.

"Hey, sleepyhead," Dan whispered awhile later, brushing his lips across her slightly parted ones. She slowly opened her eyes, looking up into a teasing face. "You fell asleep on me," he said, grinning.

"Oh, I'm sorry," Lisa apologized, sitting up and pushing her hair away from her face.

Dan's hand stopped her, then reached out to tuck a stray curl behind her ear. "You're beautiful when you're asleep," he said deeply.

Lisa blushed, realizing he must have been watching her. The question was, for how long?

"We should be getting back," Dan said with obvious reluctance. He rose and held out his hands, pulling Lisa up. Unsteady on her feet, she swayed toward him. "No, Lisa," he said firmly. After picking up the hamper, he took her hand as they walked back to the car.

The setting sun brought a chill to the air. Lisa

shivered slightly at the change in temperature, as Dan unlocked the car door. Once inside, he switched on the heater, soon warming them up.

"Do you have plans for this evening?" Dan asked. There was a strange note in his voice.

"No." Lisa stifled a yawn. "I'll probably wash my hair."

Dan's eyes momentarily left the road, glancing at her. "You still have grass in it." There was amusement in his voice.

"So do you." She grinned, turning to brush the green from his hair.

"Don't, Lisa." His hand gripped her wrist before she could reach her objective. "I don't want to have a wreck out here."

She sat back, smiling to herself, aware of her power over this man. A moment later, she leaned forward, switching on the radio to a station with soft music.

"You don't mind, do you?" She smiled at his profile.

"Not at all." One hand left the steering wheel to curl about the nape of her neck in a caressing motion. "The music is like you."

"Me?" Lisa looked up with a puzzled frown.

"Soft and warm." Dan's voice caressed her as potently as his fingers did her skin.

The rest of the drive passed quickly and Dan was soon opening the door to her darkened apartment. Lisa switched on a nearby light, and she picked up a piece of note paper propped up against a lamp. "Deb's out for the evening," Lisa said, quickly scanning the scrawled words.

"I'll say good night, then." Dan set the hamper on the table.

"Would you like some coffee before you go?" she ventured quickly. "It won't take long for me to make."

Dan walked over to her and placed his hands on her shoulders. "I don't think it would be a good idea, Lisa," he said gently. "Because we'd never drink that coffee; we'd only end up in there." He gestured toward the open bedroom door.

"Dan, I've never—I mean—" Lisa stumbled over her words, knowing her cheeks were burning.

He pressed his fingertips against her lips, silencing her. "I know," he said softly. "That's why I have to leave now. I'll talk to you later."

Dan kissed her forehead in an unfamiliarly tender gesture before turning to leave.

Sunday passed slowly for Lisa. She found herself reluctant to talk to Debra about her day with Dan. All she could think of was returning to work on Monday morning, being able to see him again.

When Monday morning finally arrived, Lisa dressed with extra care, knowing that her teal jersey dress clung to her in all the right places. She brushed her hair in loose curls about her face, pulling one side back with a decorative comb.

"That's sure to cause a few heart attacks," Debra said dryly, sipping her coffee. "Or is all of this allure meant for just one particular person?"

"The senior partners prefer the secretaries to wear dresses instead of pants," Lisa said straightforwardly.

"That's not a dress; it's a declaration of war," Debra pointed out.

"I'll see you tonight," Lisa responded, ignoring her cousin's teasing.

At the office, when Lisa sat down at her desk she found a stack of sheets waiting for her. Obviously Dan had been working the previous day. After half an hour, she looked up to see Dan stride past her desk and into his office without a word of greeting to her. The door was slammed shut behind him.

Lisa sat still, unsure whether to be angry or upset. Taking several deep breaths, she returned to her work. Twenty minutes later, the intercom line buzzed.

"Yes?" she spoke distantly.

"Miss Winters, come in here please." Dan's voice sounded cold and remote.

Lisa picked up her steno pad and pencils and took another deep breath. By the time she entered Dan's office, her face showed no sign of her feelings. She seated herself across from him, opened her pad and looked up expectantly.

"These letters have to be mailed out this morning," Dan said brusquely, without looking up. Then, barely pausing for breath, he began to dictate rapidly.

Lisa was drained by the time he had finished. "Will that be all?" she asked politely.

"Yes, except that Mr. Todd is coming in at two, and I don't want to be disturbed while he's here." He still hadn't looked up.

"Yes, sir." Lisa spoke crisply as she rose. She didn't know what he was up to, but two could play his game. She'd die before she'd let him see how much pain she was feeling.

Lisa's afternoon went by quietly while Dan was

closeted in the office with his client. Just as she was getting ready to leave for the day, the phone rang. Sighing, she picked up the receiver. "Mr. Nolan's office."

"Mr. Nolan, please. This is Morgan Grant." The woman's voice was a throaty purr.

"I'm sorry, Miss Grant," Lisa said insincerely. "Mr. Nolan is in conference with a client and has asked not to be disturbed."

"Of course, and he does get what he wants, doesn't he?" The soft laugh was pure seduction. "Would you please have him return my call? No matter how late it is."

"Of course, Miss Grant. I'll give Mr. Nolan your message," Lisa said smoothly, writing the note on a message pad. She then dropped the note on a tray that held Dan's messages when he was out of the office. Making a face at the closed office door, she picked up her purse and left.

"You've been a ray of sunshine all evening," Debra commented wryly a few hours later.

"It was a busy day," Lisa replied, shrugging her shoulders.

"A busy day or a grouchy boss—the kind you'd like to shoot?"

"It's hard to say," she sighed. "He barely spoke to me. I doubt that he even knew I was there."

"Oh, I think he knew you were there, all right."

"No, he didn't." Lisa's face wore a puzzled frown. "We're right back to where we started from when he first began working for the firm."

"Did you ever stop to think that there might be a good reason?" Debra asked reasonably.

"He probably wishes he hadn't come down from his throne to mix with a lowly mortal," Lisa said sarcastically.

"You idiot." Her cousin's voice was affectionate. "As usual, you're not thinking with your head. What's his astrological sign?"

"His birthday is in late January," Lisa replied.

"Aquarius." Debra looked thoughtful. "Let's look him up in my astrology books. They may give us a hint."

Twenty minutes later the two cousins were seated on the living room floor, each with a glass of wine, as Debra leafed through several books.

"Aries and Aquarius are quite a combination," Debra told Lisa. "You're a fire sign; he's an air sign. You think with your heart; he thinks with his head. Aquarians are known to be unpredictable, arrogant, private, brilliant and high-achieving, and to have insatiably inquiring minds. No matter what their professions, they always go far."

"What does all that have to do with Dan's attitude toward me today?" Lisa asked curiously.

"I'm just trying to help you understand him better. He's not going to be the type of man to show his true feelings about anything. He might even act the opposite of what he feels."

"Meaning today he was actually happy as a lark?" Lisa asked doubtfully. "That would be a little hard to believe."

"No, just that he's always going to be difficult to

understand. But no matter what goes on, the two of you will be in tune with each other. You might have clashes, but you'll always go back to each other. You can't fight destiny, Lee," Debra concluded. "And I have an idea your life and Dan's are going to be closely intertwined."

"I don't *want* our lives to be intertwined," Lisa protested.

"Why don't you take some advice? Go in there tomorrow and be as sweet as sugar; act as if nothing ever happened." Debra grinned impishly. "He may be baffling you, but I bet you can baffle him just as much. Give him something to think about. Besides," Debra added, "Mark never instilled those feelings in you."

"Strange, I've always felt comfortable with Mark, but with Dan . . ." Lisa's voice trailed off, as she remembered her response to Dan's kisses.

"Yeah," Debra sighed, resting her chin in her hand. "Just when we think we have them eating out of our hand, they turn around and fool us. Men!"

As the week progressed, Lisa's calm demeanor threatened to crack more and more often. Her restless nights left her with dark circles under her eyes and taut features. By Thursday afternoon, she felt ready to scream if someone said one wrong word to her. Glad that Dan was out of the office for the afternoon, she kept her mind occupied by concentrating on her filing.

"Hello, Lisa."

From her kneeling position in front of the file cabinets, Lisa looked up to find Mark standing in front of her desk. "Mark, I thought you were in Seattle until the middle of next week," she said, flashing him a warm, welcoming smile. She *had* missed him, even if she knew he could never be more to her than a friend.

"I finished early." He gazed at her with evident concern. "Are you feeling all right? You look awfully pale."

"It's been a hectic week," Lisa replied, rising gracefully, and absently smoothing the front of her tan skirt, where a long slit revealed a shapely leg. She sat down at her desk.

"Have dinner with me tonight," Mark urged. "We haven't had a chance to talk in a long time. Not since the night of the shower."

Lisa studied him, no longer seeing a man she had once thought she could fall in love with. "Mark, I—" Her carefully started refusal was abruptly cut off by a crisp voice.

"I'm afraid Miss Winters will have to refuse your polite invitation, since she'll be working late this evening." Lisa looked up into angry blue eyes. Before she could think how to reply, Mark scanned Dan's grim features.

"I see," Mark said. "Then good night, Lisa. I'll see you tomorrow."

Lisa waited until Mark was out of earshot before she turned her temper on Dan. "I don't know why you think you have the right to—"

With a quick turn of his wrist, Dan jerked Lisa out of her chair and pushed her none too gently into his office, slamming the door behind him. "Oh, Lisa, I can't care how angry you are at me," he groaned, putting one hand on each side of her as he pressed her against the door. His mouth closed hungrily over hers, giving her no chance to protest. And as his kiss deepened, he lifted Lisa's arms to encircle his neck, pulling her even closer against him. "You've been horrible to me all week," she said, out of breath, when Dan finally lifted his head, letting his lips move along her jawline and up to her ear. "I thought you had decided last weekend was a mistake."

"If I felt anything was a mistake, it sure wasn't last weekend," Dan said wryly, before his lips moved downward again to reclaim her mouth in a sweet, searing kiss. His breathing was ragged when he finally lifted his head.

"Then why the iceberg act?" she asked in a soft voice.

"Reasons," he said lazily, letting his thumb rub sensually along Lisa's ear before he bent his head to nip her earlobe. "Before I decide to make love to you here and now, why don't you invite me over for dinner tonight?" Dan's breath was warm.

Lisa was still curious to learn the reasons behind his coldness toward her, but she couldn't seem to concentrate on her anger when he stood so close to her. "You'll have to take pot luck," she murmured.

"I'll even bring the wine," Dan said huskily, again moving his lips over her skin in a sensual caress that sent shivers down her spine.

"Oh, all right."

Dan slowly released her, although one arm still loosely encircled her waist. "Does that mean I *am* invited to dinner?"

A smile curved her lips. "Seven o'clock?"

"I'll be there," he promised, pressing a hard kiss against her mouth. "Now get out of here so I can finish some of my work. I see I have to give my secretary plenty to do to keep her out of mischief."

Lisa laughed as she turned to open the door. Although Dan still hadn't explained himself, she felt better than she had all week.

Debra had left a note saying she would be out all evening, and after reading it, Lisa quickly started to boil water for the spaghetti and to get the sauce simmering on the stove. Then she hurriedly showered and refreshed her make-up. Next she twisted her hair up on top of her head in a loose knot and donned a silky pants and tunic outfit, golden beige edged in dark brown. She had just freshened her perfume when the doorbell rang.

Taking a deep breath, she walked back into the living room and opened the door for Dan, now dressed casually in a cream-colored silk shirt and dark green slacks. His eyes darkened as they took in the seductive picture Lisa presented.

"Very nice," Dan said deeply, pulling her into his arms for a lingering kiss. "It's a good thing you don't wear anything this sexy to the office, or I'd never be able to concentrate on my work."

"I have an idea that if you wanted to concentrate on your work badly enough, you could, no matter what I wore." She linked her arms around his neck.

"I brought a contribution for dinner." Dan stepped back and proffered a bottle of red wine. "Though I would prefer to stay right here, skip dinner and curl up with your very lovely body."

"That's you," Lisa teased. "All talk."

"Oh, there's action, too," Dan added wickedly. "At the right time."

Lisa turned to go into the kitchen, and Dan followed, offering to lend a hand as she put the finishing touches to their dinner of spaghetti, garlic bread and tossed salad.

Conversation was limited during their meal, though Lisa was aware that Dan's eyes never left her. Flustered by his unnerving gaze, Lisa drank more than usual. By the time their dinner was finished, Lisa's world had become a rosy haze.

"I'll help with the washing up," Dan told her, as she rose to pick up the dishes.

"Oh, no," she protested. "They won't take long at all. Just go on into the living room and make yourself comfortable."

Lisa hurriedly rinsed off the dishes and stacked them in the dishwasher. She could hear the sounds of the radio, tuned to a station with soft, seductive music.

When Lisa soon joined Dan in the living room, he was seated in an easy chair across the room. The look he flashed her was one of pure sensuality; then he rose lithely, halting long enough to switch off one of the lamps to give the room an intimate glow. Then he approached her.

"Dance with me, Lisa," he said throatily, slipping his arms around her waist to pull her against his lean body.

Lisa slipped her arms around his neck, letting herself be caught up in the slow, sensual music. She marveled at how well their bodies fitted together. Their dancing was no more than a rhythmic swaying, as Dan's lips hovered near hers. Feeling the heat rise in her blood, she raised her face, inviting his kiss.

"Lisa," Dan groaned, crushing her against him.

The wine, combined with Dan's seductive caresses, was enough to open the battle against Lisa's defenses. Dan's lips traveled along her throat to her shoulder, where he pushed aside the neckline of her top to trace a fiery trail along bare skin. But Lisa's mind was still working overtime. After a week of seeing Dan as a cold, almost ruthless man, this change in his personality was too much for her. Moaning softly, she twisted away from him. Wrapping her arms around her own body, Lisa stood with her back to Dan, trying to control the clamoring emotions within her.

"No." She shook her head. "You can't act the tyrant all week, then come here and make me forget your actions with a few kisses."

Lisa was unprepared for Dan to slip his arms around her waist and draw her back against him. "Kisses?" Dan murmured in her ear.

Lisa tried to twist out of his arms, but without success, as Dan's hold only tightened, turning her to face him. With scant effort, he picked her up in his arms and carried her over to the wide couch. He lay her down and stretched out beside her, one leg over hers. Lisa's arms curled around his neck in surrender, pulling his face down to hers.

"You taste good," she murmured against the slightly rough skin of his jawline.

"You taste better." Dan's tongue traced the neckline of her tunic top as his fingers deftly dispensed with the buttons. Lisa gasped, half in shock, half in pleasure as he teased her bare breasts. She unbuttoned Dan's shirt, letting her palms slide over his muscular chest and shoulders. Lisa moaned softly, arching her body against his.

Shuddering, Dan lifted his head to rest his forehead against Lisa's, his eyes closed. His ragged breathing was proof of her effect on him. "This is dangerous, Lee," he muttered thickly. "Right now, all I want is to make love to you. To keep you in bed for a week."

Unconsciously, Lisa wet her lips with the tip of her tongue. She was surprised that Dan's warm body was not heavy, but lay upon her as a blanket might. Her emerald eyes glowed with passion, and her body ached for a fulfillment that only Dan could assuage. As her fingers fiddled idly with his hair-roughened chest, she laughed. "I never could think of you as some stodgy old lawyer. You look at my legs too much when you give dictation."

"Um, you do have very nice legs." Dan buried his face in her hair, as his fingers pulled out the clips, letting the heavy golden tresses tumble free. "Makes me wish that mini skirts were back in fashion again, except then I doubt I'd be able to get any work done."

"Are my legs nicer than your previous secretary's?" Lisa's fingernails idly scratched his skin.

"Stop it," he moaned, grabbing her wrist to still her action. "I'm not made of steel." Smiling wryly, he buttoned her top. "Too much temptation." He straightened up, cradling Lisa against his chest.

"Well, are they?" She asked.

"Are what?"

"My legs," Lisa persisted. "Are they nicer than your previous secretary's?" She twisted her head to get a better look at his face.

"Carolyn had very nice legs," Dan mused, rubbing his hand over his jaw. "Great legs, in fact." He paused deliberately. "Especially for a woman of fifty-eight, with seven grandchildren at last count."

"Oh, you!" She punched him playfully. "Can't you ever be serious?"

"The last time I was serious was when I took my bar exam, hoping and praying the entire time that I would pass it."

"It seems to me that you didn't have anything to worry about," Lisa replied. "You've done very well for yourself in the relatively short time you've been in practice."

"It's called being in the right place at the right time. And I've worked hard every step of the way, and I still have a long way to go."

Lisa could almost hear the words he left unspoken, words telling her that he would have precious little time for anything or anyone else in his life until he reached his desired goals. It was as if he was warning her, as with the suspended lovemaking, not to become too involved with him.

"What would you do if your roommate decided to up and get married?" Dan asked suddenly.

"I don't know," she replied honestly. "Probably find myself a new roommate."

"You're a good cook, right?" He bent his head to nuzzle her ear.

"Yes."

"Know what a washer and dryer look like? And how to work them?"

"Of course." She was puzzled by the odd line his questions were taking.

"Well, then, you could always move in with me," Dan said softly. Then, muttering under his breath, he quickly pushed her away. "I shouldn't say things like that. How about some coffee?"

"All right." Lisa rose, combing her fingers through her tousled hair. She walked into the kitchen, and within a few minutes, she had the coffee pot perking. She set out a tray with two cups, a creamer and a sugar bowl.

"As usual, done with complete efficiency." Dan's voice from behind startled her. He stood in the doorway of the kitchen, leaning against the doorjamb with his arms crossed in front of his chest. "On which side of the family are you and Debra cousins?" he asked curiously.

"Our mothers are identical twins." Lisa said, glad for an excuse to keep busy, what with Dan's tall figure in such close proximity. "Deb looks like our mothers and I took after my father."

"Then there's a chance *you* could have twins," Dan murmured, his eyes on her slender figure.

Lisa's pulse quickened as her mind's eye pictured twin boys with dark blond hair and steady blue eyes. The thought was not at all unpleasant. She silently shook her head free of such thoughts. "We have some brandy if you'd like some with your coffee," she said hoarsely, turning away to pick up the tray.

"No, thanks; the coffee alone is just fine." He came forward to take the tray from her hands, and he carried it into the living room.

Seated on the couch, Lisa poured two cups, handing one to Dan. She added cream liberally to her own, reflectively watching it swirl in the dark coffee. "You never did say why you decided to join the firm," she said casually.

"They wanted a liberal to grace their ranks," Dan told her, as he sat back, stretching his long legs out in front of him. "And the idea of working with a group of lawyers, rather than alone, appealed to me." He paused. "They also made me an offer I couldn't refuse."

"Such as a partnership?"

Dan's head turned, his eyes piercing. "Either Connors told you that, or you're much smarter than I thought," he said coolly. "I have an idea it's the latter, too."

"I am very perceptive, yes. And you don't seem the type to join a firm, so I wondered about it." A smile curved her lips. "Besides, would you have told me about the offer?"

"No," he said without hesitation.

Lisa was hurt by Dan's reply, and she ducked her head to hide her expression. His hand lightly touched her chin, propelling it upward to face him.

"Poor little Lisa," Dan murmured. "Your face is like an open book, or rather, your eyes are. Those days when you were angry at me, even when you seemed so sweet and appealing, were quite a revelation. Those eyes would spit smoke and fire at me while that very lovely mouth would smile politely and phrase polite words. I used to think that you were sitting out there just hoping I'd make a mistake so you could inflict a horrible torture on me."

She laughed, surprised by his perception. "I *had* hoped, when you first came, that we'd open an office in Siberia so you'd be put in charge," Lisa confessed.

Dan set his coffee cup down, took hers out of her hand and set it down, as well. He reached over, pulled her across his lap and cradled her in his arms. "If so, I would have insisted that my very capable secretary go along with me," he growled. "The nights are long and cold up there. Not to mention lonely." Lisa couldn't hold back her giggle. "This is the way it should be," Dan told her, resting his head against the back of the couch. "We don't need to fight all the time, do we? This is much more enjoyable, isn't it?"

Content, she silently nodded, as she rested against his chest. Lisa had no idea how long they sat there in each other's arms.

"Much as I hate to break the mood, I better go," Dan finally murmured in her ear.

Lisa nodded, as she sat up and rose from the couch. At the door, Dan rested his hands on her shoulders, looking down at her upturned face. "Thank you for a lovely evening and a very good dinner," he said quietly. "I guess I'll see you in the morning."

"Bright and early." She smiled up at him.

Dan left after giving her one last lingering kiss. Lisa put the coffee cups on the tray, carried them back into the kitchen and rinsed them out. Glancing up at the clock, she was surprised at the hour. She thought briefly that it was unusual for Debra to stay out so late on a week night. Finishing her chores, Lisa went into the bedroom and, surprisingly, fell quickly asleep.

Chapter Four

Both women overslept the next morning and had to hurry to get ready for work. "No use in looking beautiful for a bunch of animals." Debra grinned, gesturing toward her jeans and T-shirt. "Lucky you, with good-looking men in and out of your office all day." She eyed Lisa's mint green, soft cotton dress appreciatively. "See you tonight. Or are you going out with Dan?" Lisa had told her about her evening with Dan as they had hurriedly drunk their morning coffee.

"Not that I know of." Lisa said, stopping in front of the mirror for one last look. She looked different. She couldn't put her finger on what the change was, but she knew she wasn't the same person she had been a few weeks ago.

Lisa was glad to have a quiet day at the office, since Dan was in court until at least late afternoon and might not be coming in at all. She was surprised when Mark stopped by her desk to ask her to have lunch with him. The pleading expression in his eyes forestalled her refusal, and she found herself agreeing to be ready at twelve-thirty.

Mark chose a well-known Chinese restaurant not far from the office. Lisa always enjoyed going there for its excellent food and subdued oriental atmosphere.

"Your boss seems to be extremely possessive concerning your free time," Mark said casually after their food had arrived.

"No, he just has a very heavy workload right now, and he wants to be able to count on me," Lisa said cautiously, as she spooned sweet and sour shrimp onto her plate. "You know how sticky that case for Mr. Jamison is. I have to be there to handle all of the minor problems that crop up."

"You may be a dedicated secretary, Lisa, but you've never been *that* dedicated." His tone was derisive. "A beautiful young woman like you needs much more. And you won't find it in an office. Or in Dan Nolan's arms."

"I don't intend finding anything in Dan Nolan's arms, Mark," she snapped, angry with the sudden overt twist the conversation had taken. "I do my job, no more. Don't think you see something that isn't there."

Lisa was spared saying anything further, when she spied a familiar figure across the dining room. Morgan Grant, followed by a gray-haired man in his fifties, walked toward them, and she flashed Lisa a cool smile.

"Well, what a surprise, Miss Winters." Morgan stood beside their table, the older man standing quietly behind her.

"Miss Grant," Lisa said in an even voice, "I'd like you to meet Mark Connors, one of the senior associates of the firm. Mark, this is Morgan Grant, a friend of Mr. Nolan's." The words seemed to stick in her throat.

Mark's look was openly appreciative as he gazed at the cool, well-groomed blonde.

"Mr. Connors." Morgan held out a well-manicured hand decorated with mauve-polished nails. "It seems that our table is now ready. It's nice to see you again, Miss Winters. Please give my regards to Mr. Nolan." Without introducing her companion, she glided away.

"Lovely woman, but she seems without a heart," Mark commented once they were alone again. "She and Nolan should get along famously."

"What makes you say that?"

"I doubt either one has one ounce of feeling in their bodies. Nolan lives for his work and I bet that woman lives for herself. They wouldn't know passion if it hit them in the face."

Lisa turned her head to hide the expression in her eyes. She would never tell Mark that she knew differently when it came to Dan. He *was* certainly capable of passion. She was surprised that Mark, normally so straitlaced, would talk so casually of passion, especially when she wondered if he knew the true meaning of the word.

After they finished lunch, they walked slowly back to the office, savoring the warm spring afternoon. When they arrived back, Mark turned to Lisa with a smile. "I enjoyed our lunch," he said sincerely. "Can I hope for dinner with you tomorrow evening as well?"

"I—I'm not sure," she said evasively. "Why don't you give me a call in the morning. I'll be home then."

Back at her desk, Lisa sighed as she sorted through the small stack of telephone messages she had picked up at the receptionist's desk.

"Glad to see you're staying out of mischief."

Startled, Lisa looked up to find Dan standing in front of her. "I thought you wouldn't be back for a few more hours," she said in surprise.

"Another postponement," Dan said grimly. "Put down on my calendar that Mr. Jamison will be in here next Tuesday at ten. If someone's already slated there, call them and reschedule." He walked back into his office.

Recognizing his tone as one of frustration, Lisa silently jotted down his instructions.

"Get me the file on Jamison," Dan called out, shrugging off his dark blue suit coat and hanging it up behind his door. He was already seated behind his desk when Lisa entered with the large manila folder. He tossed his stack of telephone messages to the other end of the desk. "Deal with these as best you can," he ordered crisply. "As far as anyone's concerned, I'm still not here."

Lisa's quiet afternoon soon evaporated as she began handling Dan's telephone messages. No one questioned her authority as she dealt with the many problems that cropped up during the course of the afternoon. By the end of the day she felt completely fatigued. But if Dan could keep up the hectic pace, so could she.

"Even slaves take a coffee break." Dan's voice interrupted Lisa's train of thought.

"Oh, I was just making a few notes." She turned around to see him leaning against the doorjamb, his tie loosened.

"Save it until Monday." Dan tiredly stretched his arms over his head. "I'll warn you now that next week is going to be very busy for both of us. Have a good weekend, Lee."

"You, too." Lisa's smile wasn't intended to lessen the sarcasm of her words. Feeling a little irked by Dan's casual dismissal, she picked up her purse and left, stopping by Mark's office first.

Caught in the act of picking up his suit coat to leave for the day, Mark was surprised to see Lisa standing in the doorway.

"Think you could buy a poor working girl dinner?" she asked brightly.

"I think I could manage that," Mark answered, matching her light tone.

"Then let's go." Lisa walked forward, taking his arm. "I'm starving!"

Lisa spent the evening being the brightest and most sparkling companion any man could wish for. So much so that when Mark left her back at her car, she felt drained of all energy.

"What would you say to dinner and a movie tomorrow evening?" Mark asked hopefully, taking advantage of her good humor.

"Why not?" Lisa flashed him a warm smile. There was no point waiting by a telephone that wouldn't ring.

"About six?"

"I'll be ready."

Mark dropped a light kiss on her lips, before watching her get into her car. Lisa started the engine, determined to fully enjoy her weekend.

Dan hadn't been joking when he said that the following week would be busy for both of them. Lisa was back to going into work early and leaving late each day. For two weeks she practically forgot what free time was. Dan was grimly determined to win the Jamison case, and he drove her almost as hard as he drove himself.

Then, on that second Friday afternoon, he called her from court, triumph in his voice. "We won," he announced without preamble.

"That's great! I'm so glad for you," Lisa said fervently.

"Then show it by celebrating with me," he said. "Be at my place at eight for a candlelight dinner. This may come as a surprise to you, but I can cook."

Lisa held her breath, unable to believe her ears. She had spent two weeks convincing herself that what had happened between them was in the past and best forgotten. "I—ah—I didn't think you would go in for that sort of thing," she said finally.

"You'd be surprised what I go in for." He gave her the address and directions. "I'll see you at eight."

When Lisa replaced the receiver, she realized that her hand was trembling.

Lisa was glad that she was able to leave the office on time that day. When she arrived home, she found Debra already there. She was frantically rummaging through the closet, muttering to herself.

"What are you doing?" Lisa asked, walking into the bedroom.

"Pat and I are going out to dinner with his parents this evening." Debra pushed her fingers through her hair. "And I can't find my green crepe."

"Obviously you forgot that you took it to the cleaners yesterday." Lisa was amused to see her usually composed roommate acting so distraught.

"Then what am I going to wear?" Debra wailed.

"Go take a shower, do your hair and fix your make-up." Lisa pushed her toward the bathroom. "I'll lay out a dress for you. What time is he picking you up?"

"Seven."

"Then you better hurry. I'm not meeting Dan until eight." She had hesitated about telling Debra she was having dinner at Dan's apartment, but the other girl seemed so preoccupied that she hardly noticed.

An hour later, Debra's dark hair was twisted intricately on top of her head, and she wore a simple black gown with spaghetti straps.

"Seductive, yet wholesome enough for meeting a man's mother," Lisa said, smiling. She turned, hearing the doorbell. "That's probably Pat. I'll get it."

Lisa opened the front door and smiled at the dark-haired man standing there. "She's just about ready," she told him. "Come on in."

Pat's eyes lit up as he looked past Lisa's shoulder. "Now that is some dress," he said appreciatively.

Debra picked up her stole and evening bag. She flashed an uneasy smile at Lisa. "See you later."

"Just relax," Lisa whispered. "You'll be fine."

After Debra left, Lisa showered in a hurry and changed into a pair of teal linen pants and a gauzy teal-and-gold-print tunic top. She brushed her hair and clipped one side back with a tortoise-shell comb. Smiling to herself, she dabbed perfume onto her pulse points.

Lisa found Dan's apartment building easily, and she parked her car in front. As she approached the front door, she could feel the butterflies fluttering in her stomach. Her hand hesitated for a second before she knocked. Just before her courage deserted her, the door opened to reveal a casually dressed Dan in a dark brown shirt, with the cuffs neatly folded back, and tan pants.

"Right on time." He stood aside to let her pass. "Come on in."

"This is very nice." Lisa looked around the spacious living room, decorated in shades of green.

"Care for a tour?" Dan asked, adding wickedly, "of course there isn't much besides the bedroom."

"Oh no, that's all right," she said hastily, turning around to see the mockery in his eyes.

"I enjoy getting a rise out of you. You blush so beautifully." He gestured toward the couch. "What would you like to drink?"

"Vodka and tonic." Lisa's eyes turned toward the small dining table, already set, complete with two candles in silver candlesticks. The thought of whether or not Morgan Grant had ever come here for dinner flashed through her mind. She decided that she didn't care to find out the answer, not just now.

Dan disappeared for a moment, then he reappeared carrying her drink in one hand and a glass of whiskey in the other. Handing Lisa her drink, he sat down beside her and held up his glass. "To the Jamison case."

Lisa smiled sunnily as they clinked glasses together in a toast. "I'm flattered that you asked me to celebrate your triumph with you."

"You were the one who kept all my notes in order for me and who typed my briefs over several times," Dan told her. "Therefore, you deserve not only some of the credit, but part of the reward." His hand reached over to toy with a stray curl that hung over her shoulder. "Such beautiful green eyes," he mused. "I never imagined that anyone's eyes could have such vivid color."

Lisa felt mesmerized by his steady gaze.

"I better check on dinner." Dan stood up abruptly, breaking the spell, and walked into the kitchen.

Lisa hastily gulped her drink to restore her composure. "Is there anything I can help you with?" she called out.

"No, thanks; I haven't blown up a kitchen yet," he replied.

Dan walked back, carrying a tray into the dining room, and he set the serving dishes on the table. Lisa stood up and walked over to him. "Smells good," she said brightly.

Dan held her chair out for her, then he lit the candles. After pouring the wine, he sat down across from her.

Lisa found the roast chicken cooked in wine sauce delicious, as well as the wild rice and the tender vegetables. "You weren't joking when you said you could cook. This is terrific." She smiled at him.

"Actually, I'm usually better at hamburgers and

steaks on a barbecue," he confessed. "But I enjoy experimenting every once in a while."

Lisa had an idea that this was a man who wasn't too eager to give up his freedom. She wondered what Morgan Grant thought about that.

"It was an excellent dinner and I insist on helping you with the dishes," Lisa told him.

"Don't worry about the dishes," he assured her. "I have a cleaning lady coming in tomorrow. She'll do them. Would you like a brandy?"

Lisa wandered around the living room, stopping to study a painting on one of the walls near the fireplace, while he filled two small snifters.

"Here you are."

She turned, smiling, to accept the glass Dan held out to her. "Thank you." Her smile faded as she visualized the same scene with Morgan Grant in her place.

"Is something wrong?" Dan looked at her with concern.

"No." She shook her head.

Dan snapped off one of the nearby lamps, leaving only a lamp in the far corner lit." "That's much better." He grinned, taking the drink out of Lisa's hand and setting it down.

Lisa's mouth parted under Dan's sensual onslaught. His hand pressed against her lower back, molding her closer to him. Why was he doing this? Why was she here celebrating with him instead of Morgan?

"This isn't right," Lisa muttered against Dan's mouth. "You just assume I'll give in to you because I'd be afraid for my job otherwise."

Dan's hand gripped her forearms in a bruising hold. "Is that what you think?" he demanded roughly. "Then perhaps you'll understand this better." His punishing kiss was meant to leave Lisa without time to think. He used all of his expertise, demanding a response whether she wanted to give one or not.

Lisa emitted a soft moan under the hard pressure of Dan's mouth. At that, Dan's kiss gentled, but Lisa still wasn't given any time to think. She was hardly aware that she had begun unbuttoning Dan's shirt, splaying her fingers over his bare warm skin, or that Dan had maneuvered her over to the couch, lowering her to the cushions. Lisa obligingly shifted her position to give Dan room to lie down beside her.

"Soft and warm. Just what I need on such a beautiful night," Dan murmured, burying his face in her hair, as his fingers deftly dispensed with the tiny buttons of her tunic top. "You always smell so fresh and flowery," he muttered as his lips traveled down to her bare breasts.

Lisa gasped at the intimate touch.

Dan looked up and cradled her face between his palms. Her shimmering green eyes looked up at his glazed blue ones. Lisa lifted one hand, using her fingertip to trace his face. Dan grabbed her wrist, slowly moving her hand toward his mouth. Keeping his eyes on her face, he moved his lips over her sensitive palm and up to each fingertip.

"I wish I could understand you," Lisa murmured.

"Then the challenge would be gone." He flashed her his crooked grin.

Lisa linked her arms around his neck, burying her face against his warm skin. This was what she wanted. To be in Dan's arms, touching him, kissing him. Each time she was with him, her inhibitions faded a little more.

"It's hard to keep any self-control around you, lady," Dan said thickly. His tongue traced the outline of her ear, sending disturbing sensations to the pit of her stomach. "No man in his right mind could resist such a beautiful woman," he muttered. His lips moved back to capture hers in a long and drugging kiss.

Lisa's head whirled in a kaleidoscope of colors. Dan's hands were confident as they moved over her body. She knew it would not be long before her inhibitions would be totally swept away. Her body moved restlessly against his, emotions exploding within her.

Releasing a deep breath, Dan finally untangled himself from Lisa and sat up. Dazed from their lovemaking, Lisa lay back against the cushions. Suddenly aware of her semi-naked state, she flushed, fumbling with the buttons of her tunic. Dan turned his head and, seeing her feeble efforts, pushed her hands away, deftly dealing with the many buttons himself.

"You're very tempting to have around the house," Dan said wryly. "Too tempting, in fact."

Lisa sat up, pushing her hair away from her face with a trembling hand. "I—I should get going," she said shakily.

"No, you don't," he said firmly, rising to his feet. His shirt was soon buttoned and tucked into his pants. "I'm going to get us some coffee, and we're going to talk."

"Talk?" Lisa echoed.

Dan looked down at her upturned face. His fingers again traced the outline of her slightly parted lips. "*Talk.*" He stressed the word.

"I'd like to comb my hair first," she told him.

"Around the corner to your left."

Lisa picked up her purse and went into the bathroom. The bright lights snapped her out of her dazed state. Her hair hung tousled about her face, and her eyes were large emerald pools. Lisa tentatively touched her lips, swollen from Dan's passionate kisses. She stared fixedly at her reflection, unable to believe that the person she was looking at was herself. She slowly opened her purse, taking out her hairbrush. Within a few minutes Lisa's hair had been brushed back into order, and she had put colorless gloss on her lips. On the outside she had been restored to order, but she knew she would never again be the same on the inside.

When she returned to the living room, Dan had set two steaming cups of coffee on the coffee table.

"Thank you," she said hoarsely, sinking down on the couch, but leaving some distance between them. She had already discovered how potently Dan's nearness worked on her senses.

"It won't be the same between us from now on, Lee," Dan told her. "I think you know it, but you don't want to admit it."

"You seem to hide your own feelings very well," she replied.

Dan leaned back tiredly, resting the palm of his hand against the back of his neck. "I believe in burying myself in my work. That's all I feel I need." His voice sounded almost bitter.

Lisa felt a shooting pain in the vicinity of her heart. Who or what had made Dan so bitter about any type of lasting commitment?

She was distracted as Dan began talking casually to her, just as if they hadn't just shared such passionate moments. But pulled into the conversation, Lisa lost track of the time, as they discussed various topics unrelated to their relationship.

"I really must be going," Lisa suddenly said, realizing the hour, and she stood up. "I thank you for having me for dinner. I enjoyed it."

"And I enjoyed you," Dan murmured.

Lisa ducked her head, picking up her purse.

"I'll walk you to your car." Dan grasped her hand.

Outside, the night air cooled Lisa's heated cheeks. Dan stood next to her as she unlocked her car door.

"I'm driving down the Coast tomorrow," he told her, before dropping a light kiss on her lips. "I'll see you on Monday."

"All right." She smiled as Dan closed the car door after her.

As she drove away, Lisa could see Dan in her rearview mirror. He wasn't walking back to his apartment; instead he was walking along the sidewalk, his head bent down, as if in thought.

When Lisa arrived home, she found Debra there ahead of her. "Was your evening a success?" Lisa asked.

"It was great. Pat's parents are both very nice," Debra replied. "And I'm going to take him home with *me*, one of these weekends. How was your evening?"

"We had dinner and just talked," Lisa replied casually, taking a nightgown out of her dresser drawer.

"Lee, does Dan realize how you feel about him?" Debra asked quietly.

Lisa sat on the edge of Debra's bed and slowly shook her head. "No, and I can't let him know either," she said in a low voice. She wasn't even sure how she felt herself.

"So what are you going to do? Stay there working for him and wait around for him to pay real attention to you?"

"I don't know what I'll do," Lisa said bleakly. "All I can now do is take a day at a time. Dan's as much as said that he doesn't want a lasting relationship. And he seems very definite about it."

"Don't they all." Debra laughed, then sobered. "I wish I had a ready answer for you, but I'm afraid I don't. Maybe something will come up to change things."

Lisa merely nodded as she got ready for bed. But sleep was a long time in coming.

Chapter Five

When Lisa arrived at the office Monday morning, she was surprised to find an envelope on her desk with her name written across the front. Curious, she turned it over, slitting it open with a letter opener.

"What on earth?" A large tortoise-shell hair comb fell onto the desk top. Lisa's cheeks burned as she realized it was the comb she had worn Friday night to Dan's apartment. It must have fallen off and she hadn't even realized it. She looked inside the envelope, but there was no note. Lisa replaced the comb in the envelope and put it away in her purse.

Dan came out of his office just an hour later.

"I found the comb on my desk this morning," Lisa greeted him. "Thank you."

"Found it on the couch," Dan said, glancing through his stack of mail. "Don't put any calls through until I say otherwise," he ordered, walking into his office.

Lisa's days soon formed a pattern. Dan had thrown himself into a new case, and he spent a great deal of time closeted in his office or away in court. Morgan called daily, and she was frequently at the office when Lisa left for the day. The other girls had disappeared. She supposed there was a limit even to Dan Nolan's energy. Lisa bitterly realized that Dan rarely asked her to work overtime anymore and rarely did so himself. And the triumphant expression on Morgan Grant's face every time she left arm in arm with Dan was enough to cause Lisa to clench her teeth, frustrated and angry.

One Friday afternoon, Mark stopped by Lisa's desk, smiling warmly. "How about having dinner and going to a movie with me this evening?" he asked her.

"Thanks for the invitation, but I'm so tired that I think I'll just go home and fall into bed," she said sincerely.

"Then how about tomorrow night?" Mark asked, persisting.

Lisa hesitated for only a second. Why should she sit home in misery because of Dan's obvious preference for Morgan's company? "I'd like that very much."

"Great. I'll pick you up at eight." He walked away, as Dan walked out of his office and watched Mark leave.

"Do you have that correspondence for Wilmer finished?" Dan asked crisply.

"Naturally." Lisa picked up several typed sheets and handed them to Dan.

"Confident of yourself, aren't you?" he queried.

"How else could I manage to put up with you, Mr. Nolan?" she asked with mock innocence.

"There will come a day, Miss Winters," Dan murmured, as he walked back into his office, "when you will find yourself in a situation where you won't be so confident." Turning back, as if something had just occurred to him, he asked, "What are your plans for this weekend?"

"Nothing earth-shattering yet." Lisa shrugged her shoulders. "Cleaning out the closets has never been one of my favorite tasks."

"I'm planning on driving down the Coast Sunday. Care to come along?" Dan's offhand invitation was surprising.

Lisa nastily asked herself whether he had asked Morgan first and if she had refused. But she knew she couldn't turn him down. "I'd like to, yes." Her voice was just as casual.

"I want to get an early start, so why don't I pick you up at eight? We can stop somewhere on the way for breakfast. Dress casually." Dan glanced toward his paper-laden desk and grimaced. "You've worked late enough and, as far as I'm concerned, so have I. Come on; I'll walk you to your car."

When Lisa arrived home a half hour later, she found the apartment empty. A note propped up against a living room lamp informed her that Debra had gone out for the evening. Obviously Pat meant a great deal to her, judging by the amount of time she had been spending in his company lately.

Glad to have the apartment to herself, Lisa decided on a long and leisurely bubble bath, then went to bed with a good book. Sleep came easily for the first time in weeks.

Lisa was ready on time Sunday morning. She needed no mirror to tell her how beautiful she looked. Her brief white shorts and cotton shirt in muted stripes of pale blue and green showed off her golden complexion to its best. Her make-up was sparse, just a light application of blue eye shadow to her green eyes and some honey-colored lip gloss.

"Now that's an outfit I really like," Dan said greeting her appreciatively. "I always said that I was a leg man."

"I should think though that you'd like to have some things left to your imagination," Lisa teased.

"I do, but there are times when it's nicer to have the view to enjoy." He added casually, "How was your evening with Connors yesterday?" So he had heard Mark asking her out!

Lisa hid a smile that threatened to appear. "Very nice, thank you," she said indifferently, walking toward Dan's car.

After a quick breakfast, Dan drove along the Coast through the many small towns that only came alive during the summer. Now, in early spring and with schools still in session, they were not as crowded as they would be in another month or two.

"On days like this, I just want to get away from everything," Lisa said lazily, as she looked out the car window. "To steal away from the world."

"Curl up with a good book? Do your own thing?"

"Exactly. Where are we going?"

"Down around the Dana Point area," Dan said, naming a popular beach spot.

Almost an hour later they drove past the boat-filled channel that marked the Dana Point Yacht Club. Then Dan turned onto a winding road that led to the hills overlooking the ocean. In front of a modernistic house of reddish-colored wood, he slowed the car. Lisa got out and looked at the house in awe. Even though the house appeared plain on the outside, it was arresting. Two stories tall, it had a sloping roof, giving it an angular appearance. The windows were narrow rectangles and many-paned. Lisa thought that the house must be quite new, since the surrounding land hadn't been landscaped yet. Without grass and flowers, the house appeared stark and lonely against the background of bright blue sky, yet not unappealing.

"It's fantastic," she said honestly. "How did you ever find such a beautiful house?"

"In my head," Dan replied offhandedly.

"Your head!" She was amazed. "Do you mean you designed this yourself? That it's *your* house?"

"That's right. You didn't know that I wanted to be an architect once, did you? It took me over four years to have it built, but it was worth it." Dan looked around with an expression of self-satisfaction on his face. He stood, his legs apart, hands on his hips. "Come on; I'll take you on a tour." He turned and held out his hand.

Smiling, Lisa took his hand and walked with him toward the front door, as he took a key out of his jeans pocket.

Inside, she looked up at the beamed cathedral ceiling and the skylight that allowed sunshine to light up the house. Stairs of polished wood wound upward to the second floor.

"The bedroom is upstairs," Dan explained, leading her into the living room.

Lisa looked around, noting the simple oatmeal-and-dark-brown tweed sofa and a large stone-lined fireplace. She walked over to the sliding glass doors that opened onto a patio fenced in only at the sides. There was a spectacular view of the ocean, which was only a short distance away. A tiled Jacuzzi tub could be seen in one corner of the patio, with its own wrought-iron fence around it. As with the front yard, the patio still had an unfinished look about it, as if waiting for someone to come and fill it with flowers and shrubs.

"I didn't want to lose the view, but I did want the privacy." Dan walked up behind her. "This way I can have both and not lose anything in the bargain."

Disconcerted by his nearness, Lisa moved away, exploring the remainder of the downstairs. She smiled with approval at the large kitchen, with its huge wood-grained cabinets and a butcher-block table in the center of the room. The kitchen appliances were an almond shade, a complement to any decor. The adjoining dining area held a small oval table with four dark green leather chairs. In the next room, Lisa saw a desk and book-lined shelves.

"You don't even get away from your work here, do you?" Lisa gestured toward the room.

"Actually, I can get a lot more done around here because of the peace and quiet. Care to see the rest of the house?" Dan stood looking expectantly at her, as if waiting to see what her answer would be, and that answer seemed important to him.

Lisa knew that the remainder of the house meant the

bedroom upstairs, and her curiosity was aroused, even though she wished it wasn't. She nodded, following Dan toward the stairs, and she slowly climbed them behind him.

The sloping roof of the house gave the one huge bedroom a loft-like effect. The bed's headboard consisted of shelves built into the wall that were filled with books. Lisa walked over to get a closer look at the titles. She turned to Dan with a puzzled frown.

"Gory murder mysteries are great for putting me to sleep," he said, explaining, as he grinned.

Lisa looked down to the cognac-colored velvet comforter. "It's a water bed." She gave a laugh. "It took me a moment to realize why it looked so funny."

"You act as if you've never seen a water bed before." Dan walked over to lean against a chest of drawers.

"Only in stores." Lisa put out a tentative hand, testing the gently rolling motion.

"Why don't you sit on it?" he suggested.

Lisa shot him a wary look as she gingerly sat down, feeling the bed not only yield to her slight weight but roll with it as well. "It's very comfortable," she giggled as she flopped backward, her arms outspread like a small child's. "But couldn't you get seasick on this?"

"Depends on what you're doing?" he replied suggestively.

Lisa sat up abruptly, her enjoyment gone. She understood Dan's meaning only too well. She wondered, with a touch of bitterness, how many women had been on this bed before—in Dan's arms.

"You should feel flattered, Lee." Dan's voice was maddeningly casual, as walked over to the sliding glass doors that opened onto a balcony. "I guess you could say that I consider this house my inner sanctum. I've never brought anyone here before. Just you."

"Oh? I should think the solitude and the view would be perfect for romantic trysts." Her voice was sharper than she had intended. "I bet the bedroom has a spectacular view of the sunset. Or would it be the sunrise?"

Dan walked over to sit on the edge of the bed. His hand reached out, fingers combing her hair away from her face. "Is that why you think I brought you here? To make love to you?" he asked quietly, solicitous. "To wear down your defenses with a water bed and a view?"

"I don't know." Lisa sighed wearily. "I don't know what you want from me."

"I had this house built in hopes of eventually being independent enough to work from my home. That's why there's an office downstairs. And I own enough of the surrounding land to comfortably add on to the house when the time comes," Dan told her. "I brought you here because I thought you would enjoy the ride and wouldn't read anything into it. You're very relaxing to be with, Lee. You don't demand that I make conversation all the time or that I be constantly amusing. I wasn't planning a seduction, just a leisurely drive." Dan's fingers were creating disturbing sensations as they moved against Lisa's skin.

"I'm sorry," Lisa said softly, now contrite, as she lifted her eyes to his face. "As usual, I jumped to the wrong conclusion."

Dan leaned toward her, brushing his lips against hers. Once, twice, three times. Lisa's arms circled his waist, allowing him to pull her against him. It wasn't long before they lay on the bed, kissing each other lightly, murmuring softly to each other.

"You're very comfortable to cuddle up to," Lisa whispered.

"Like a teddy bear?" he teased quietly.

"I like teddy bears." Her eyes closed as Dan's lips brushed over each eyelid. "They're a little girl's best friend. And they keep nightmares away."

Lisa was willing just to lie in Dan's arms, feeling his lips brush occasionally against her hair, her forehead, or her lips. If she had been asked later what they had talked of she wouldn't have remembered. The talk was nonsensical, gently teasing and tender. She didn't remember that she fell asleep, only that her eyes kept closing more and more often and then refused to open right away.

When Lisa awoke later, the room was dark, surrounded with early evening shadows. She found that her head was now resting on a pillow and that she was curled up on her side, her favorite position for sleep.

"Is it my brilliant personality or my enlightening conversation that seems to put you to sleep whenever we're together?" Dan asked Lisa this in an amused voice. "This could give me an inferiority complex, you know. I never thought of myself as being a bore."

"Actually, it was because I had to get up so early this morning," she replied, sitting up and pushing her hair away from her face.

Dan was standing with his back to the sliding glass doors, watching Lisa with an undefinable expression on his face. He walked over to the edge of the bed.

Grasping her wrists, he gently pulled her upward. "That's a dangerous place to stay, Lee," he said quietly. "We probably should be going. We can stop for dinner on the way back."

"I'm not exactly dressed to go anyplace fancy," Lisa said, gesturing at her brief shorts and shirt.

"That's no problem," Dan assured her, leading the way down the stairs.

As they walked outside, Lisa turned for one last look at the house, framed now in orange light from the setting sun. She wistfully wondered who would eventually live in the house with Dan. Who would be lucky enough to share his bed—his dreams—his life?

"We'll go into town and find a place to eat there," Dan said, as they got into the car. "How about some Mexican food?"

"Sounds great."

Over dinner, Lisa learned more about Dan's experiences in law school. He mentioned a little about his family, who lived in Washington state, yet he still seemed to impart little information about himself.

"What changes would you make in my house?" Dan asked suddenly, leaning back lazily in his chair, one arm draped over the back.

"None," Lisa said without hesitation.

"None?" He looked at her with disbelief. "Oh, come on; anytime a woman sees a house, she automatically wants to do it over."

"Not me. The house suits you. It *is* you," she replied quietly.

An hour later, as Dan's car sped along the highway, Lisa sat back in her seat, reflecting on the day. Despite the length of time she had known Dan, he still remained an enigma, jealously guarding his private life. She wondered if she would ever learn more about the man beneath his aloof exterior.

"Dan, what about—" Lisa's voice froze, as she gazed ahead at a set of wavering headlights that seemed to be coming straight at them. "Dan!" Her scream tore from her throat as he sharply turned the wheel in the opposite direction. Then everything went black.

When Lisa came to, she was lying in the dirt. As she sat up she was aware of sharp pains shooting through her head. Disoriented, she looked around and saw Dan's car in flames. As her memory cleared, horror washed over her in cold, alarming waves.

"Dan!" Lisa looked frantically around until she found a still figure lying prone near a tree. She staggered to her feet and ran over to him. Dropping down on her knees, Lisa carefully turned Dan over and cradled his head in her lap.

"Anything I can do to help, Miss?" A man with a concerned expression on his face approached her. "I called for an ambulance and it's on the way. Is your friend all right?"

Lisa looked down at the profusely bleeding gash on Dan's forehead and at his torn jeans, which exposed a deep, jagged wound on his leg. "Oh, please, darling, be all right," she tearfully pleaded with the unconscious Dan. "You have to be all right." Tears flowed down her cheeks.

Lisa was barely aware of when the ambulance arrived. The attendants helped her inside and then strapped Dan onto a cot, carefully carrying him to the ambulance.

"He's going to be all right, isn't he?" she asked one of the attendants, uncaring of her own cuts and bruises.

"Don't worry, lady; he'll be fine," he reassured her. "You just relax. You've had a bad shock, too."

Once in the emergency room, Lisa helplessly watched an attendant roll the still-unconscious Dan away for treatment. A nurse approached her, taking her arm to steer her toward another examination room.

"Can't I stay with him?" Lisa asked the nurse. "Please?" Her eyes were eloquent in their pleading.

"Why don't you let the doctor look you over first?" the nurse suggested gently. "You've got some nasty cuts and bruises we need to take care of."

Lisa kept up her pleading to the doctor as he carefully checked her over.

"I'm keeping you here for a couple of days," he informed her, as he scribbled busily on a chart.

"Me? I'm all right," Lisa protested.

"I'd like to make sure of that before releasing you," he answered.

"What about Mr. Nolan? Can't I please see him? He *is* all right, isn't he?" she asked persistently.

The doctor hesitated momentarily before answering. "Mr. Nolan is now in surgery. He has some internal injuries, but we're taking care of things now."

Lisa could feel hot tears filling her eyes. She remembered Dan's pale and still features as he lay by the burning car. The doctor leaned down, patting her shoulder in a comforting gesture.

"Look, I'll let you know about your boyfriend as

soon as I find out," he said kindly. "It's going to be awhile, so why don't we get you to your room so you can rest? We've already notified your cousin. We found her number in your wallet."

Finally feeling the effects of the sedative the doctor had administered earlier, Lisa could only nod her head wearily. The nurse brought in a wheelchair and Lisa was soon installed in a hospital bed, fast asleep.

Even with the sedative, Lisa's sleep was marred by recurring dreams of the auto crash. Once, she even sat up in bed, screaming in fear. A nurse was quickly by her side, murmuring soothing words in comfort.

"Dan, Dan is hurt. Badly hurt," Lisa muttered, shaking her head from side to side as she was pushed gently back against her pillow. "Please help him."

"Your friend is all right, dear," the nurse quietly assured her. "But you need to get your rest. I'll stay with you until you can fall asleep again."

Lisa closed her eyes, barely aware that the nurse lifted her wrist to take her pulse. Knowing Dan was all right was the only medicine she needed, allowing her mind to slip back into oblivion.

When Lisa awoke again, the sun was shining brightly through the curtains. Slowly opening her eyes, she saw a dark-haired figure seated in a chair by the window.

"Deb?" Her voice came out in a croaking whisper.

Debra rose swiftly and came to Lisa's bedside. "How do you feel?" she asked, looking down with a smile.

"As if my mouth had been stuffed with cotton and they forgot to take it out." Lisa grimaced.

Debra poured some water into a plastic cup, then held it to Lisa's lips, supporting the back of her head as she lifted her up.

"Do they know how it happened?" Lisa asked after Debra set the cup down.

"A drunk driver." Debra looked disgusted. "Of course, he didn't have a scratch on him. The police have him in custody. You were lucky in being thrown clear, though. The car burned completely. The gash on your arm took eight stitches, but there won't be any scar to speak of."

"How is Dan doing?" Lisa asked hoarsely.

"He's listed in critical condition, Lee. It looks like he won't be back to work for awhile."

"All because he wanted to show me his house," Lisa whispered to herself.

"His house?" Debra looked puzzled, then she decided the medication must still be affecting Lisa's thought processes. "The doctor said I'm not to stay very long because I'll overtire you. I brought you a couple of nightgowns and some make-up. Also some magazines and books." She smiled fondly at Lisa. "Look at the bright side, Lee. Three doors down this hall you have a captive audience to work your charm on. Take advantage of it. *Full* advantage. I'd better go before the nurse comes in and throws me out. I'll be back tomorrow."

Surprising herself, Lisa easily fell asleep again. When she woke up that afternoon, the doctor was entering her room with a nurse.

"Well, you certainly look much better than you did last evening when you were brought in." He smiled at her. "How are you feeling?"

"My head still aches a little, and I feel as if my throat was lined with cotton wool," she admitted.

The doctor adjusted his stethoscope, listening to

Lisa's heart, then checked her pulse. "You're a very lucky young woman," he commented, making notes on her medical chart. "In fact, if the tests and X-rays come out the way I expect them to, I'll discharge you the day after tomorrow."

Lisa shook her head, uninterested in her own well-being. "How is Mr. Nolan doing?" she asked. "Is there a chance that I could see him? Talk to him?"

"He's been taking a long nap. You can see him tomorrow for a few minutes. He's been asking for you." The doctor smiled. "Right now he still needs peace and quiet. You can get up tomorrow for some exercise, but don't go running in any marathons for awhile."

After a light dinner, Lisa lay back against her pillow, leafing idly through a magazine. She was unused to lying around and doing nothing. The accident now seemed a hazy dream to her, except for the throbbing of her arm and the ache at her temples. Then she remembered Dan lying motionless near the burning car. The ugly wounds. She shuddered, remembering the frightening scene.

The following morning, with the assistance of a kindly nurse, Lisa took a shower and washed her hair. Then she changed out of her cotton hospital gown and into one of her own nightgowns and a powder blue robe. A touch of make-up helped hide the paleness of her features. Because of the pain in her arm, Lisa settled for just brushing her hair away from her face, securing it with a clip.

"Think you'd like to take a short walk now?" the

nurse smilingly suggested. "At least down the hall a little ways?"

"I'd like to very much." Lisa's face lit up.

Quietly entering a hospital room very much like her own, Lisa viewed the patient in the bed with growing alarm. An i.v. bottle was set up next to the bed, with a tube leading down to Dan's arm. A white bandage was over one eye. His head slowly turned at the sound of a visitor, and a faint smile broke over his pale features.

"Hi," Dan greeted her in a voice huskier than usual. "I'm sorry that I'm causing you to use your sick leave sooner than expected."

"I'm just glad you're all right." Lisa's voice throbbed with concern. "They wouldn't tell me very much. I was so worried about you."

"I'm doing fine. Do you think they'll let you stay for awhile?" Dan gestured weakly toward the chair near the bed. His eyes strayed toward the bandage on Lisa's arm, visible just below the short sleeve of her robe, then upward to her face, with a questioning look.

"Eight stitches." Lisa laughed it off. "They're only keeping me for some tests today." Her voice dropped to a low whisper. "They said that you were critical. That you had been badly hurt. You were so still out there."

Dan's eyes caught her in a compelling gaze. "I'll be fine," he said quietly.

Lisa's hand tentatively reached out, gently touching the scratches on Dan's exposed arm. "They said it was a drunk driver." Her voice could barely be heard. "He didn't even get hurt."

"Just think of the beautiful day we had," Dan told

her. "I'm just glad you're all right." The expression on his face changed abruptly. "I wouldn't have wanted anything to happen to you."

"I think you better let Mr. Nolan get some rest," the nurse said, quietly entering the room. "You also have to go down to have some X-rays taken now."

Lisa stood up and impulsively leaned down, dropping a light kiss on Dan's lips.

"I'll enjoy being an invalid if I can keep getting attention like this," he murmured as she straightened up.

"I'll see if I can come back later," she promised with a smile.

"Don't worry. I won't be going anywhere," he said wryly.

Glad that Dan felt well enough to joke, Lisa was able to smile more naturally at him.

She was eating her dinner later when the doctor walked in with a broad smile on his face. "Good news," he greeted her. "No signs of internal injuries. I don't see any reason why you can't leave tomorrow as long as you make sure to take it easy when you're home."

"I'm glad to hear it. But what about Mr. Nolan? I know he'll have to stay here longer, but is he doing all right?"

"He's doing just fine, but he'll be here for at least ten more days. Of course," he grinned, "from the looks of his visitor he may get better a lot sooner. The blonde in there with him now doesn't seem the type to play nurse for too long."

Lisa's spirits sank; the doctor had to be talking about Morgan Grant. She certainly hadn't wasted any time!

Dinner suddenly seemed very unappetizing. She had thought of going down to visit Dan after she had finished eating. Now it was the last thing she wanted to do. She couldn't bear to see Morgan Grant hovering over Dan, speaking to him in that seductive voice of hers.

After trying to concentrate on a television program she didn't care for, Lisa finally switched off her light. It was a long time before she fell asleep, and even then there were tears on her face.

The following morning, Lisa was up early, dressed and ready to leave before Debra arrived. She had just finished packing her overnight case when someone appeared in the doorway.

"Hello, Miss Winters." Morgan's voice was cool and distant. "I understand that you were with Dan in the accident. I must say, you were very lucky."

"Yes, I guess I was," Lisa said matter-of-factly, snapping the case shut and turning to face the other woman.

Morgan stood at ease, cool and elegant in a silver-blue suit of raw silk. "I've known Dan for a long time, Miss Winters." Her voice was conversational, as if they were discussing nothing more important than the weather. "And I won't allow some little nobody of a secretary to take him away from me. Dan and I have an excellent relationship. Stick with that Mr. Connors. He seems to be more than interested in you. Dan isn't for you."

"I think I'll just leave that decision to Dan, if you don't mind," Lisa said calmly.

"As far as I'm concerned, there will be no repeat of

this conversation. The next time I'll take more drastic action." Morgan turned and left the room.

Lisa sat down on the bed before her trembling legs could collapse beneath her. She now knew that war had been declared. She also knew that Morgan would do anything in her power to discredit Lisa in Dan's eyes, if Lisa didn't follow the other woman's advice. The implications were frightening.

"Ready to go?" Debra asked gaily, breezing into the room with a nurse pushing a wheelchair behind her.

"Definitely," Lisa said fervently.

Debra picked up Lisa's suitcase. "Do you want to stop by to see Dan before you leave?"

"No, I believe he's occupied right now." Lisa's voice sounded cool, and she was amazed at her own self-control.

"I peeked in his room on my way over here, and he was all by himself." Debra was surprised by Lisa's sudden change.

Lisa chewed thoughtfully on her lower lip. She glanced up at the nurse. "Would you mind waiting a few moments?"

"Of course not." The nurse smiled cheerfully.

Lisa hurried down the hall, afraid, now, of finding Morgan in the hospital room. She heaved a sigh of relief on seeing that Dan was alone.

"So they're going to let you out?" Dan greeted her with a smile.

"Yes, Deb's here to take me home." She returned his smile. "I just thought I'd come in to say good-bye."

"I should think that would be a little difficult since we do happen to work together," he said dryly. "Perhaps you could find the time to visit your old boss before he gets discharged."

A smile curved Lisa's lips. "If you'd like me to."

"I would—very much," Dan said quietly.

"I'll be able to go back to the office a week from Monday, so I'll try to hold things together," she told him, aware of the rapid way her heart was pounding. "I better go before Deb comes looking for me." She turned to leave.

"Lee?" She turned at his questioning tone. "No good-bye kiss?" There was a hint of a wicked gleam in his blue eyes.

Flushing deeply, Lisa leaned down and dropped a kiss on Dan's cheek.

"I know you can do better than that, but I'm afraid I'm not in a position to argue," he said wryly.

"Take care, Dan," she said softly, before leaving the room.

Lisa was quiet during the drive back to the apartment. Her thoughts were back with the man lying in the hospital bed, and with the blonde-haired woman who would make sure to be with him, keeping anyone away who might distract his attention from her.

During the next few days, Lisa discovered that she still needed to rest. The day after she came home from the hospital, she was lying on the couch, reading, when the doorbell rang. Puzzled as to who it could be, she was surprised to find a delivery boy, who handed her a colorful bouquet of flowers arranged in a straw basket.

She slit open the envelope and read the card with a smile.

From one comfortable teddy bear.

After raising the bouquet to inhale the sweet fragrance, Lisa set the flowers down on the table where she could easily see them during the course of the day.

Chapter Six

That Saturday, Lisa drove to the hospital to see Dan. Unsure whether Morgan might be there, and not wanting another confrontation with her, Lisa cautiously peeked around the door.

"Why not come in all the way?" Dan's amused voice called out.

Lisa's startled eyes darted over to the window, where Dan was seated in a chair, a book in his lap. "You're up," she said inanely.

"They don't believe you should lie around too much after surgery," he explained. "Don't worry, I'm not able to chase you around the bed yet."

"Thank you for the flowers," she said softly. "But don't you think that *I* should be sending them to *you?*"

"I'd feel pretty silly getting flowers." Dan grinned, then sobered. "How's your arm?"

"It's stopped throbbing." She sat down in a nearby chair. "Have they said when you can go home yet?"

"The end of next week," he replied, grimacing as he shifted his position. "The first thing I'll have to do is look for another car. Mine isn't fit for more than the junkyard anymore."

"Is there anything you need?" Lisa asked.

"No, thanks; I've got a supply of murder mysteries to keep me occupied." Dan gestured toward a small stack of paperback books. "What have you been up to?"

"I'm trying to get my energy back. I feel ridiculous getting tired so easily," she admitted. "I'll be glad to get back to work on Monday." Her voice drifted off, as she realized that Dan wouldn't be there.

"I guess I'll have to keep in touch by phone until they let me go back to work again," he told her, then launched into a series of instructions for Lisa to follow during the next week.

"Trust you to keep on working no matter where you are." Morgan's throaty voice came from the doorway. Her eyes were as cold as ice as they rested on Lisa. "You must be very conscientious to come out here on a Saturday, Miss Winters."

Only Lisa could hear the faint mocking undertones in Morgan's voice. "I'm sure Mr. Nolan will tell you that we have a very heavy workload," Lisa murmured, hurriedly rising to leave. "Well, I'll be going. I'll keep you informed of anything important that may come up, Mr. Nolan," she said formally.

Dan's eyes were puzzled as he looked up at her set features.

"Now, darling, you're supposed to be convalescing, not worrying about your work," Morgan scolded prettily, entering the room. "Miss Winters should be ashamed of herself." She turned to Lisa with false solicitude. "You're looking quite pale yourself, dear."

"Yes, I'm sure I am." Lisa's eyes refused to waver from the other woman's steady gaze. "Good-bye, Mr. Nolan. I'll be sure to keep the office in good order for you." She turned to leave.

"Good-bye, Lisa." Dan's quiet voice followed her out of the room.

When Lisa reached her car, she sat behind the wheel, unsure whether to cry or laugh. It appeared that Morgan would get her way after all. Lisa suspected that she was a vindictive enough woman to do whatever was necessary to achieve her aim.

Lisa was glad to get back to work on Monday, even without Dan there. When she arrived at her desk, she found Mark there ahead of her.

"You're looking fine, Lee." He smiled warmly. "I'm sorry I didn't get to come by and see you. You know how hectic things get around here."

"I'm afraid I spent a great deal of time sleeping, anyway," Lisa replied. "The pain pills the doctors give you these days can really knock you out."

Mark glanced around, as if to make sure that there was no one within earshot. "It's suprising that you and Nolan were together that day."

"You don't have any claim on me, Mark." Lisa's voice was a warning.

"I just don't want to see you get hurt, Lee," Mark said quietly.

Lisa smothered a laugh. Those were the exact words Dan had used regarding Mark. Was either of them truly concerned about her welfare? She was beginning to doubt it.

"We heard that Nolan will be discharged a week from Friday if all goes well. He'll rest at home for a while before returning to work though." Mark added sarcastically, "I guess he'll want you to work there during that time."

Lisa looked down at the week's accumulation of mail on her desk. She was anxious to get rid of Mark and get back to work.

"I think I'd better get back to earning my salary." Her crisp voice was a dismissal. "It's amazing how things pile up when you're away for more than a couple of days. I'm afraid Mr. Nolan is going to have his work cut out for him when he returns." She sat down in her chair.

"I'll see you later, Lee," Mark said, and left her alone.

Lisa found the office quiet with Dan not there. Her only contact with him was over the telephone several times a day. Although he hinted that she should come down for a visit, Lisa chose to ignore him. She didn't care to run into Morgan again, not so soon anyway.

Anxious to keep her thoughts away from Dan, Lisa accepted several lunch and dinner invitations from Mark, much to his surprise and delight.

"I have a special place I'd like to take you to this evening for dinner," Mark told her one Friday over lunch. "I think you'll enjoy it."

"Then I'll make doubly sure to look extra special for you," Lisa said lightly, as she glanced at her watch. "Oh, oh; I'd better get back to the office. I'm late now."

When Lisa arrived back at work, she found a message telling her to call Dan at an unfamiliar telephone number. She dialed; the line rang only twice before it was picked up.

"Nolan here."

"Dan, it's Lisa. I got your message." How could she sound so calm when her pulses were pounding just at the sound of his voice?

"They finally turned me loose," he told her. "I thought that you would take pity on me and come over and cook dinner."

"I'm sorry, Dan, but I have a date this evening," Lisa tried to keep her voice light when all she felt inside was dismay.

"Oh? With Connors?" Dan asked sharply.

"Yes." To keep her hands from trembling, she picked up a pencil and idly doodled on a scrap of paper.

"I see," he said flatly.

No, you don't see at all, Lisa thought miserably to herself.

"I'd appreciate it if you'd come over here for a few hours on Monday afternoon," Dan said crisply. "About one."

"I'll be there," she said softly.

"Have a good weekend, Lee." Dan hung up.

Lisa set the receiver down, feeling oddly like crying. She had a good idea that Morgan would gladly go over to Dan's and fix dinner for him instead. An intimate dinner for two.

"I hope she's a horrible cook," Lisa whispered miserably to herself by way of consolation.

She felt curiously flat that evening, as she dressed for her dinner date with Mark.

"I've seen more enthusiasm for your semiannual trip to the dentist," Debra commented, watching Lisa apply her make-up.

"I'm just tired, that's all." Lisa moved to the closet to take out a floor-length skirt with its blue-gray and matching print chiffon blouse.

"How's Dan doing?" Debra asked deliberately.

Lisa's fingers hesitated momentarily before they continued buttoning the tiny pearl-gray buttons on the front of the blouse. "He was discharged from the hospital today," she said, finally.

"Why didn't you go back again to see him at the hospital, Lee?" Debra asked. "You said he asked you to."

"It was very hectic at the office, trying to get caught up with all the work," Lisa said unconvincingly.

"Dan wouldn't have minded if you got a little further behind with your work. Besides, you had the time to go out with Mark, and you haven't been staying late at the office," Debra quietly pointed out. "And I know it can't be because of Morgan Grant. You've never been worried all that much about competition before. And you can't say that the chemistry isn't there between you and Dan."

"I'm not frightened of anyone," Lisa said evenly, applying perfume to the base of her throat. "Dan

Nolan doesn't encompass my life, that's all. I'm living my life the way I prefer to."

"Liar," Debra said softly, turning to answer the door as the doorbell pealed. "I bet Mark still doesn't provide any fireworks, either."

Lisa was glad to get away from Debra's disapproving eyes and sound observations when Mark arrived.

"I won't tell you to enjoy yourself," Debra murmured, so that only Lisa could hear.

"Don't wait up for me," Lisa answered sweetly as she swept out the door.

"You look beautiful tonight, Lee," Mark said, his dark eyes lighting up in frank appreciation. "I feel flattered that you went to all this trouble for me."

"I just believe that when a woman is out with a good-looking man she should look lovely enough to ensure that he keeps his eyes on her," Lisa replied with a warm smile that didn't quite reach her eyes.

She was glad she had dressed with such care when Mark pulled up in front of an elegant restaurant known for its excellent cuisine. Inside, they were seated on red velvet chairs in the dining room. "This is lovely, Mark," she enthused, keeping her eyes on the menu.

"Don't look at the prices," he grinned. "After all the years I've practiced law, I can certainly afford to take my special girl out for a fancy meal now and then."

Lisa felt alarmed by Mark's statement. She was beginning to fear that he might be reading more into their relationship than she was prepared to accept. And the last thing she wanted to do was hurt him.

Lisa hadn't expected their dinner to be anything but excellent, and she wasn't disappointed. Afterward they drove to a nearby club to listen to a band Lisa had barely heard of, though Mark seemed quite familiar with their music.

"What would you say about going back to my place for a nightcap?" Mark asked as they left the club.

"It's terribly late, Mark. I should be getting home," Lisa told him.

Without protest or argument, Mark drove back to Lisa's apartment house. "Then how about inviting me in for coffee?" he asked, unable to keep his eyes off her face.

"I'm sorry, Mark, but it's so late, and I'm sure Deb's already asleep." She smiled gently. "Another night."

"Are you going to be home this weekend?" he asked.

"I should be."

"Then I'll call you." Mark took her in his arms, bringing his lips against hers. Lisa let her body melt against him, responding as much as she could. All the while, though, she was comparing the emptiness she felt now with the way she felt when Dan kissed her.

"I—I really have to go in now," Lisa said shakily, pulling away from his embrace. She knew that if she had been with Dan, instead of with Mark, he would never have let her go so easily. He would merely have smiled and pulled her back into his arms again. And she would have gone willingly. "Thank you for a beautiful evening."

Inside the apartment, a light burned dimly in the

living room. Lisa noticed a note propped up against the lamp.

Lee,
    Dan called and asked that you call him if you get in halfway early.

                                                    Deb

Reading the note, Lisa began to feel anger growing within her. "Who does he think he is that I'll jump when he snaps his fingers?" she muttered, tearing the paper into small pieces and letting them drift to the floor.

Feeling tense, she went into the kitchen and poured herself a glass of wine. She leaned back against the counter, staring off into the darkness as she sipped it. The more wine she drank, added to the wine she had had at dinner and at the club, and the more she thought about Dan's message, the angrier she became. Glancing up at the kitchen clock she noticed that it was past three o'clock. There was a dangerous gleam in her emerald eyes as Lisa set her wine glass down on the counter and picked up her evening bag.

A few moments later she guided her car out of the parking lot and down the deserted streets. With Dan's address firmly in her mind, she drove across town.

Twenty minutes later, Lisa parked her car in front of Dan's apartment building. Humming softly under her breath, she reached his front door and pressed her finger against the buzzer, holding it there until the door was angrily wrenched open.

"What the—!" Dan's scowling eyes raked Lisa's innocently smiling features.

"I know that you asked that I return your call, but it was much easier just to come over." Lisa swept haughtily past him and into the apartment.

"Do you know what time it is?" Dan demanded, moving his fingers through his tousled hair.

Lisa looked up at him with innocent eyes. "Oh, I'm sorry. Did I wake you? I guess I didn't think of the time." Her eyes moved to the cane Dan was leaning heavily on. "By the way, how are you feeling?"

"Better than you will in a while," he dryly replied. "You're drunk, Miss Winters."

"I don't get drunk, Mr. Nolan," Lisa said haughtily, unaware that she was standing a little off balance. "Now, what did you want to talk to me about?"

"Lee, it's quarter to four in the morning." Dan sat down on the sofa arm. "How was your date?" he asked suddenly.

"Very nice. Mark took me to a very elegant French restaurant." Lisa wandered aimlessly around the room, unable to keep still. "Then we went to hear a band at a nearby club."

"And what is Connors like on a date?" His narrowed eyes never left her restless figure as he spoke.

"He's very nice. Quiet, easygoing, entertaining—in short, good company."

"The kind of man you could walk all over in a minute," Dan commented shrewdly. "And he'd never say a word to stop you. If you said no to him, he'll just smile and accept it without even trying to change your mind."

"You're not being very polite tonight, or should I say this morning?" Lisa spun around, facing him with angry eyes. "You haven't even offered me a drink."

"You've had enough. How about some coffee instead?"

"Did Morgan cook dinner for you tonight?" she asked artlessly.

"No."

"Why not?"

"I didn't ask her to."

Lisa idly examined a ceramic figurine on a nearby table. "Why didn't you?"

Dan released a heavy sigh of frustration. "Because I didn't care to. I had asked *you*, and you were busy. Look, Lee, I am very tired. Why don't you go lie down on my bed and I'll bunk out here on the couch? We can talk in the morning, after you've had some sleep."

"Is it a water bed?" she asked boldly.

"No," he replied in a weary voice, knowing he wouldn't be able to reason with her.

"Poor Dan. No water bed," Lisa said in mock sadness, then she began laughing. A moment later, she stopped abruptly and grabbed the back of a chair for support. "Are we having an earthquake?" She looked at him, wide-eyed. "I feel carsick." Her voice dropped off.

Jumping to his feet, Dan swiftly guided her to the bathroom and tactfully left her alone.

For the next half hour, Lisa felt as if she wanted to die. After splashing cool water on her face and patting it dry, she walked slowly back into the living room.

"Feel better?" Dan asked from the couch.

"I'm still not sure," she muttered.

"I made some coffee for you. It might help." He indicated the steaming cup on the table in front of him.

Lisa picked up the cup with shaky hands, lifting it to

115

her lips as she walked over to a nearby chair to sit down.

"You look very lovely tonight, in spite of yourself" Dan said quietly. "I hope he appreciated it."

"Dan, I . . . I don't know what to say," Lisa said in a low voice, refusing to look up from her coffee cup. "I feel like such a fool."

"We all do something foolish at least once during our lifetime." He grinned. "I'm glad I was around to see yours."

Lisa's face reddened. She set her cup down and stood up stiffly. "I should be going. I really am sorry for interrupting your sleep."

"Don't be so hard on yourself, Lee," Dan said gently.

"I don't ordinarily do this." She shook her head, unable to look at him.

Dan stood up, grabbing his cane. He walked slowly toward Lisa until he stood in front of her. "Do you feel well enough to drive?" he asked quietly. She mutely nodded her head. "Then make sure to take some aspirin before you go to bed so you won't feel so bad when you get up later."

As Lisa opened the door, she turned, looking at him quizzically. "You never did say why you called."

Dan flashed her his crooked grin. "Maybe I was hoping your boyfriend would stand you up."

Lisa winced inwardly. "Good night, Dan," she said throatily.

"Lee." He put out a restraining hand to halt her exit.

"No–o" she moaned, twisting away from his grasp, fearing his intent. Lisa was afraid she wouldn't be able to hide her feelings from Dan much longer.

Dan's expression hardened at her reaction. "Does he mean that much to you?" he demanded.

Lisa bit her lip to still its trembling. How could she tell him that *he* was the one who meant so much to her? She still felt so unsure where Dan was concerned. "Yes," she lied, unable to look up at him.

"I'll see you on Monday, Miss Winters." Dan's voice was as cold and impersonal as it had been so long ago.

Lisa fled, not wanting him to see the anguish on her face. Instinct alone guided her home through the early morning haze. When she arrived at the apartment, she found the lights blazing and Debra pacing the floor.

"Where have you been?" Debra cried out when Lisa let herself in. "I have been worried sick and thinking the most horrible things." She stopped short, seeing the tears on Lisa's cheeks. "What happened to you with Mark?"

"It wasn't Mark." Lisa gulped back a sob. "I went to see Dan."

"Dan? But why did you go see him?" Watching Lisa's face crumple, Debra walked over to her and put her arms around Lisa's shoulders. "What happened, Lee?" she asked gently.

Lisa couldn't hold back her tears any longer. The words came tumbling out, some virtually incoherent, as she told Debra about Dan, his house, her fears for his life after their accident, and Morgan's conversation with her at the hospital. Debra led Lisa over to the couch, sitting her down. Lisa continued talking about her drive to Dan's apartment and what had happened there.

"It looks to me like you have two options," Debra said finally, after Lisa finished her story.

"What are they?" Lisa asked, raising her tear-stained face.

"One, you can continue seeing Mark, find a luke-warm happiness with him and lose Dan to Morgan; or two, you can continue dating Dan, break through his defenses and learn his exact feelings for you. If they're genuine, you've gained something wonderful; if not, then you'll have to patch your wounds and go on living. The latter is a great gamble, but it could be a very worthy one. It's up to you."

"Just because you have something so wonderful with Pat doesn't mean it can happen so easily for others," Lisa sniffed.

"No," Debra said honestly. "But you won't find out unless you try. Why don't you go to bed, sleep as late as you need to, and then try to relax over the rest of the weekend? It won't do you any good to worry. Everything will right itself in due time."

Lisa smiled mistily. "You're right," she agreed, rising to her feet. "I'll worry about it all when the time comes."

Chapter Seven

Monday morning, Lisa busied herself getting together the papers that she would bring to Dan. She still felt uneasy about seeing him again after that painful and embarrassing evening. She wasn't sure what his attitude toward her would be. She was glad that she was meeting Mark for lunch, since his undemanding presence would enable her to forget her fears for a short time. And luckily, she was able to do just that. Except she was also reminded of something else. Dan had been right. She could so easily walk all over Mark. He was always so eager to please her, never acting on his own preferences. Lisa led the way and Mark followed willingly, without questioning, something Dan would never do. His self-assurance wouldn't allow it. With him, life would always be more challenging, exciting, more alive. And more painful.

"Hey, wake up." Mark said, laughingly snapping his fingers in front of her face. "Look, why don't I pick you up at Nolan's and take you out to dinner tonight."

"No!" Lisa's voice was sharper than she had intended. As Mark looked at her with surprise, her voice softened. "I mean, I don't know what time I'll finish, Mark. It would be better if I just stayed home and relaxed this evening."

"I should feel jealous, knowing you're going to be in that man's apartment, alone with him," he said in a teasing voice. "Knowing how sexy you look today."

"There isn't any reason for you to feel jealous," Lisa told him. She was beginning to regret deceiving him. If only she could fall in love with him. It would make life so much easier. But she couldn't. And yet she didn't want to tell him the truth because she didn't want to lose his friendship.

That afternoon, Lisa drove to Dan's apartment feeling more than apprehensive. Taking a deep breath, she gathered together the file folders and got out of her car.

She opened the front door when Dan replied "Come in" to her hesitant knock. He was seated at a desk in the corner of his living room, reading through a sheaf of papers. He barely glanced up as Lisa entered and dropped the folders on a nearby table.

"I set up a typewriter for you on the dining table," Dan said crisply, still not looking up from his work. "There are some rough drafts of letters I need to have out today."

"Yes, sir," Lisa murmured.

Dan glanced up, and if he noticed the way Lisa's lemon-yellow silk dress clung to her slender frame and the way the seductive slits at the sides revealed shapely legs, he gave no indication. She could have been wearing a baggy sweatshirt and jeans for all the attention he paid her.

Lisa sat in front of the typewriter, inserted a blank piece of paper and began typing words at random to get the feel of the machine. Moments later, she was busily typing the stack of work Dan had left her.

During the course of the afternoon, Lisa found it difficult to work with Dan in such close quarters. His form-fitting jeans and T-shirt lent a casual atmosphere to the work, which she wouldn't have felt in the office, but she also found the intimacy distracting and disturbing.

Lisa's frame of mind didn't improve when the phone rang and the caller was Morgan. Dan got up, murmuring that he would take the call in the other room, and, using the cane, he limped out of the living room. He left the door slightly ajar, however, so Lisa could not help but hear some of the conversation. And judging from Dan's intimate tone, she knew that Morgan had him more in her power than Lisa had thought. The knowledge left her bitter.

"We might as well quit for now," Dan announced when he reentered the room.

Lisa sat back, flexing her tired fingers. She stood up, gathered together the letters she had typed and gave them to Dan to sign.

"Just send them out in the morning mail," he told her as he scrawled his name across the bottom of each letter. "And I'll see you again tomorrow afternoon."

"Of course. Anything else?" Her manner was that of an efficient secretary as she picked up the papers, shoved them into a folder and moved toward the door.

"Yes." Lisa had been unaware that Dan had followed her to the door. His hands gripped her shoulders, turning her around. Before she could protest, his mouth covered hers in a mind-shattering kiss. Lisa's hands couldn't help but grasp his shoulders to keep her balance. When Dan finally lifted his head, his eyes had that dangerous glitter she knew only too well. "Good night, Miss Winters," he said smoothly, the even tenor of his voice seeming to indicate that the kiss had not affected him one bit, while she felt as if the earth had been swept away from under her feet.

"G–good night, Mr. Nolan." She silently cursed her voice for trembling.

"One more thing." Dan's voice followed her out the door. "Since you'll be working here on and off for the next few days, I'd appreciate it if you'd wear something less sexy. If you come to play . . . well, that's different."

Her face flaming, Lisa wanted only to escape. As she drove away, she noticed Morgan arrive. The knowledge that the lovely Morgan, who had driven up in an expensive foreign sports car, would be spending the evening with Dan didn't help her mood any.

When Lisa later let herself into her apartment, she found Pat seated on the couch, looking through a magazine.

"Hi," he greeted her. "Deb invited me to dinner."

"I didn't expect you back," Debra said, walking out of the kitchen with a towel.

"I do happen to live here," Lisa said dryly, setting her purse down on a chair.

"I just thought you'd be at Dan's apartment, cooking him a cozy dinner for two."

"I'm sure Morgan will manage something." She couldn't keep the bitterness out of her voice.

"How was he toward you?" Debra asked.

"Like a boss with his secretary, nothing more." Lisa preferred to forget Dan's kiss at the door. "I know where I stand now. Behind the desk."

Lisa was silent during dinner, barely listening to the happy conversation between the two lovers. Unable to bear seeing two people so happy with each other, she escaped to the bedroom after the meal. Seated cross-legged on her bed, not really hearing the radio, Lisa came to her decision. From now on, she would think of Dan as her boss, nothing more. She hated the thought of using Mark as a shield, but she would badly need one. His undisguised affection was just what her faltering ego sorely needed.

For the next few days, Lisa kept up a remote front when she worked at Dan's apartment. If he was surprised by her sudden change in manner, he said nothing. Lisa even arranged for Mark to pick her up at Dan's one evening to help keep up her pretense. She also made sure to greet Morgan with an almost friendly manner. The knowledge that she was there every evening with Dan after work stiffened Lisa's resolve not to allow him to hurt her.

Lisa was glad that Dan spent a majority of his time in court once he returned to work. On the few occasions when he was in the office, she would sometimes turn to find him gazing at her with a faintly puzzled expression, but his eyes would shift as soon as he noticed her attention on him.

One afternoon Lisa returned from lunch to find Morgan seated in Dan's office, alone. "Dan had a quick conference with someone," Morgan coolly informed her. "I'm so glad we have a minute to talk alone. I'm also glad that you took my advice about Dan."

"I didn't take your advice, Miss Grant." Lisa's voice was equally remote. "I'm living my life the way I wish to."

"I'm sure you'll be much happier with your friend Mark," the other woman said confidently. "You should marry him, have children, the type of life I'm sure you really want."

Lisa's reply was cut off as Dan appeared. "Morgan, what a pleasant surprise." He smiled warmly at her.

Shaken by Dan's warm greeting to Morgan and by Morgan's words to her, Lisa went back to her desk feeling physically ill. She knew she had left the field open to Morgan and hated herself for it.

As the days passed, Lisa became even more grateful for Mark; his continued presence helped her to hide her own anxieties. As the time for the annual office picnic, held at the Phoenix Club in Anaheim, approached, she knew she would not enjoy it. It would provide a real test of her ability to act nonchalant with Dan, and she was very much afraid she would fail.

Lisa was glad to have the evening before the picnic to stay home alone, as Debra was going out with Pat.

"What time is Mark picking you up tomorrow?" Debra asked her.

"Nine or therabouts." Lisa shrugged her shoulders.

"Will Dan be there?" Debra asked pointedly.

"I didn't ask," Lisa wearily replied. "We don't talk very much except about business matters. In fact, we haven't for some time. The only time he says anything close to being personal is when he makes a sarcastic remark about Mark."

"Sounds like a case of jealousy. What does he say?"

"He claims that I walk all over Mark," Lisa said angrily.

"Mark does seem to give in to you a lot," Debra said carefully. "Tell me, Lee, are there any fireworks yet?"

Lisa's head shot up, her eyes blazing. "Aren't you afraid you're going to be late?" she snapped. She walked into the bathroom, slamming the door behind her.

"I'm only thinking of you, Lee," Debra called after her. "You can't be angry with me for speaking the truth. All you're going to end up doing is hurting Mark and hurting yourself. You can try and tell me that you don't care, but I know differently."

Lisa stubbornly stayed in the bathroom until she heard Debra leave with Pat. And, after a quiet and lonely evening spent washing her hair and manicuring her nails, she crept into bed for a restless and dream-filled sleep.

Since the day was hot and sunny, Lisa chose to wear brief tan shorts and a brown strapless stretch top under a brown-and-green print shirt left open and tied at the waist. She pulled her hair into pigtails, making herself look much younger.

Mark showed up in light blue shorts and a matching T-shirt. "You look too young for my peace of mind," Mark said wryly, viewing the lithe figure before him.

"You're not exactly in your dotage," Lisa teased him, using words she had used before, turning to pick up a brimmed straw hat to protect her face from the hot sun. "Shall we go?"

"Don't forget to say hello to your boss for me, Lee," Debra daringly called after her from the bedroom in a deliberately casual voice.

Lisa's mutinous mood had not improved by the time she and Mark arrived at the large park. Mark carried a large container of salad Lisa had prepared and set it on an already heavily laden table. Turning, Lisa greeted her secretary friend, Barbara, also casually dressed in shorts and a T-shirt.

"Would you take a look at the fashion plate who showed up among us mortals?" Barbara nudged Lisa slyly. "And you'll have to see this to believe it. Everyone is out at the baseball diamond."

Lisa followed Barbara past a large grassy area, taking a dirt path that led to a dusty baseball diamond. Nearing the bleachers, her green eyes widened at the sight of Morgan, immaculately dressed in white designer jeans and a pale rose-colored silk shirt, with a wide-brimmed straw hat protecting her porcelain features.

"Can you imagine wearing white to a picnic?" Barbara hissed. "Actually, I'm surprised she even came. I thought she was above us working people."

"I'm not surprised," Lisa said softly, letting her eyes

wander toward the baseball game in progress, settling on one jeans-clad figure whose dark blond hair glinted in the bright sunlight.

Frank, Barbara's husband, urged Mark to join the game, as Lisa and Barbara walked toward the bleachers. Morgan acknowledged their presence with a cool smile, but she said nothing. Barbara rolled her eyes at Lisa as if unable to believe what she was seeing.

Lisa was totally miserable by the time the baseball game had ended. She held in her excited cheers each time Dan hit the ball, cheering only for Mark. She was aware of Dan's glittering blue eyes watching her on occasion, but she refused to turn her head in his direction.

After the game, Mark and Lisa walked across the grass, his arm a leaden weight across her shoulders.

"We thought we'd get up a basketball game after we eat," he told her.

"And I suppose I'm expected to sit there and cheer on all of you big he-men," she said sullenly.

"Lee, I'm not going to abandon you for the entire day." Mark's voice was instantly contrite. "You know that I wouldn't do that to you."

As Lisa's head shot up, she was aware that Dan was standing nearby; he had obviously overheard their conversation. The expression in his eyes told her only too plainly that he wouldn't have put up with her childish temper. Defiantly, she tossed her head and walked on, with Mark following her. Lisa knew that she was acting childish, but she was past caring.

"Did you have a fight with Mark?" Barbara whispered later, as the men moved off for their basketball game. "Though I can't see why he would fight with you.

He thinks the world of you. Everyone knows how he feels about you."

"Oh, I don't know," Lisa sighed. "I guess it's just the sun or something. I'm going for a short walk. If Mark comes looking for me, please don't tell him where I've gone. I'd really rather be alone."

"All right; maybe the walk will help."

Lisa moved off, walking through the trees. After going a short distance, she leaned against a tree, staring off into space, trying to sort out her thoughts.

"Run off to pout?" A familiar voice sounded behind her.

Lisa turned to face Dan, defiant. "No; to be *alone*," she said sharply.

"You don't want to be alone, Lee," Dan said softly.

"Yes, I do, so why don't you just go away!" she cried out, clenching her fists at her sides. "Go back to Morgan. After all, she wants you and you want her. That's only obvious."

Dan's eyes glinted like angry blue gems as he pulled her roughly toward him. "Does this mean I want her?" he ground out before pressing his mouth against hers in a brutal kiss. He was angry with her, Lisa knew. Yet, why should he be angry? Lisa could feel the tears filling her eyes when Dan finally released her. For long moments they stood staring at each other, breathing hard.

Lisa's hand lifted; she wanted only to hurt Dan, but his reflexes were too quick for her, and he firmly grasped her wrist.

"You don't want to do that, Lee," he said quietly. "Hurting me is the same as hurting yourself."

"You have Morgan; isn't that enough?" Lisa asked in a choked voice.

Dan stood still, his eyes studying her tense features. "Yes, I guess it is," he said finally, before he walked away.

Lisa watched him disappear, wanting only to call him back. She dashed away her tears with the back of her hand, waiting only long enough to compose herself before returning to the others.

Back at the picnic, Lisa sat down next to Barbara to watch the basketball game. Dan's tall figure was easy to spot. It was obvious that he had played basketball in college and that he probably still played occasionally. And he seemed to have no residual problems from the surgery at all. Lisa noticed this, as her eyes stayed on him instead of on Mark.

Lisa felt as if a wire had been coiled inside her body, ready to spring out at any moment. It was as if her body knew something was about to happen, but wasn't sure what. Or when.

Barbara noticed; and she kept glancing over at her friend's stiff figure. "Did your walk help any?" she asked.

"Yes, in several ways," Lisa said cryptically, as she watched, tense, as Mark and Dan spoke together. What were they talking about? The wire inside her coiled tighter.

"Lee," Mark said. Her face was a carefully composed mask when he approached her. "We've been asked to join Dan and Morgan for drinks after we leave here."

Panic washed over her in a flood. No! She couldn't go

through with it! And she wasn't going to, not if she had her say.

"Mark," Lisa's voice was sweetly wheedling, "I think I left my hat back at the table. Would you be a darling and get it for me?" She cocked her head to one side, a smile lighting up her face.

After he disappeared, she quickly searched out Dan, and she was lucky to find him alone. He had shed his shirt during the basketball game and was pulling it back on when Lisa approached him.

"I don't think it would be a good idea for us to join you for a drink," she said right off. "And I'm sure you can come up with a suitable excuse."

"Why should I?"

"Because I won't do it," Lisa said through clenched teeth.

"So?" Dan shrugged his shoulders indifferently.

"I will *not* sit in some bar with you," she angrily protested, her temper beginning to run away from her. "Because then I'd have to be polite to you. And the *last thing* I want to do is be polite to *you.*"

Dan looked down at her angry face with maddening calm, as he slowly tucked his still unbuttoned shirt into the waistband of his jeans. "Forget it," he said finally, moving around her and walking off without a backward glance.

Lisa spun around, dying to throw something at his broad back. Her fierce anger still hadn't dissipated when Mark returned, carrying her hat.

"Ready to go?" he asked her.

"As ready as I'll ever be," she ground out, snatching the hat out of his hand and walking away.

"Lee, do you feel all right?" Mark was all concern as

he caught up to her. "You've been acting strangely all day."

Lisa tried to be contrite. There was no reason to take her anger out on Mark. "I'm sorry, Mark; I don't know what's wrong with me," she said wearily.

Since they were too casually dressed for many of the cocktail lounges, they chose one that was small, with a friendly atmosphere.

Now feeling sorry for her earlier actions, Lisa decided to make up for them by being sweet to Mark. She was aware of Dan's derisive gaze and Morgan's triumphant one, but she refused to back down now. When Lisa requested a second drink, she looked at Dan, finding his eyes on her with an unreadable expression. Recalling the night when she had breezed into his apartment, she hastily muttered that she didn't need another drink after all. She sat back in her corner of the booth, simmering quietly.

"We must get together some evening for dinner," Morgan said silkily.

Lisa looked at the other woman, knowing only too well that the invitation was a false one. "That does sound like a lovely idea," she echoed insincerely, as Dan's eyes narrowed.

When Morgan softly reminded Dan of a previous dinner engagement a few minutes later, Lisa heaved a sigh of relief.

"You know how Uncle is on punctuality," Morgan reminded Dan as they got ready to go, and she stole a sly glance at Lisa.

"Yes." Dan was leaning back in his seat, studying Lisa's face. "We're talking about getting together for some more weekend games, Connors. You should join us," Dan said by way of good-bye. He flashed Mark a faint smile. To Lisa he said, "See you on Monday."

She merely nodded, refusing to look up.

"How about some dinner?" Mark suggested once they were alone.

"All right." Lisa didn't feel very hungry, but she wasn't too eager to go home right away, either.

After a quick meal, Mark took Lisa back to her apartment. He stood at her door, looking at her with a strange expression on his face.

"I don't understand quite what is going on," he said quietly. "Or what it will do to us, but I want you to know that I'll always be there when you need me, Lee. Because I love you. It's as simple as that."

"Oh, Mark." Her eyes shimmered with tears; her hand reached up, cupping his cheek in a tender gesture. "How can someone as sweet and wonderful as you want only half a person?"

"That's where you're wrong." He smiled, leaning forward to press a light kiss on her lips. "I'll talk to you later when you feel more like yourself. Maybe we can have dinner again some evening soon."

Lisa entered the empty apartment feeling on the verge of tears. She had known that Mark was very fond of her, but she hadn't realized he actually loved her. She smiled grimly. It looked like Dan had been wrong: Mark was willing to marry her after all.

To keep herself busy, she did her laundry, piling the clothes in a basket to carry them down to the laundry room. When that chore had been completed, she decided to scrub down the bathroom, ignoring the late hour. By the time she dropped into bed, she was too exhausted to care that, at that moment, Dan and Morgan were undoubtedly still together.

"Lee! Lee!" Lisa tried to raise her head, her eyes squinting in the sudden light. "Lisa, wake up!" The persistent voice wasn't going to give up.

"Wh–what's wrong?" Lisa muttered, propping herself up on one elbow and pushing her hair away from her face. "Is something wrong, Deb?"

Debra shook her by the shoulders, alternately laughing and crying. "Oh, Lee, Pat just asked me to marry him, and I said yes!"

Fully awake now, Lisa broke into a wide smile. "How wonderful!" She hugged her cousin. "Tell me all about it."

"He said if he didn't ask me now he didn't know when he'd get his courage up again." Debra's green eyes glowed with happiness.

"Well, when do you think—have you set a date?" Lisa's words tumbled out in confusion.

"Three weeks from today."

"Three weeks! That barely gives us any time," Lisa protested. "How can you expect us to have everything ready in so short a time?"

"I'd marry him tomorrow if I didn't know how much it would disappoint Mom. I have no interest in a big wedding. All I want is Pat."

"Your mother is going to be ecstatic." Lisa said.

"She sure is. We called Mom and Dad tonight," Debra told her. "You and I also have strict orders to come home next weekend to begin the preparations."

"Oh, Deb, I'm so happy for you." Lisa threw her arms around her, her eyes filled with tears. "You'll be such a beautiful bride." She drew back. "I know one thing for sure, if we only have three weeks we're not going to be getting much sleep. I'll see about taking my vacation time now. I'll ask Dan first thing Monday." At the mention of his name, the light in her eyes dimmed.

"I thought we could begin working on the guest list in the morning," Debra said hastily, silently wishing that Lisa could find the same happiness she was now experiencing. "Pat's coming over with his share of the list at about eleven, and he has promised to take us out for a celebration brunch."

When the lights were switched off, much later, Lisa lay in her bed, tears streaming down her face. She was happy for Debra, but she was also envious. She wondered when her turn for happiness would come, and with whom.

Monday morning, as Lisa took the morning mail in to Dan, she decided it was as good a time as any to voice her request.

"Dan, I'd like to ask a favor," she began hesitantly, aware of his cold, mocking look. "Debra is getting married in three weeks and, if possible, I'd like to take my vacation after this week, for two weeks, to help with the preparations. Naturally, I'll make sure to have caught up with all my work." She nervously clasped her hands, as she waited for his reply.

Dan leaned back in his chair, taking his time to study Lisa's tense figure. "It took a lot for you to ask that, didn't it?" he asked softly. Then he sat quickly forward, picking up a pen. "You'd better call a temporary agency today. Just make sure they send someone capable. I won't put up with some dim-witted female who doesn't know a pencil sharpener from an inter-com."

"Thank you." Lisa's low voice was barely audible.

"Don't thank me!" Dan said harshly. Then he added, in a softer voice, "Give her my congratulations. I hope she'll be happy."

Lisa escaped to her desk, surprised by Dan's reaction to her gratitude. She wished she could understand such a complex man. But that would be like asking for the moon. Impossible.

Chapter Eight

Friday night, after work, Lisa and Debra headed up the Coast to Ventura, to the homes where they had both grown up. A few hours later, they pulled up in front of a wood frame two-story house.

"See you in the morning," Debra said to Lisa, as Lisa took a small overnight case out of the back of the car. "Mom and I will be over about ten or so."

Debra's small car then roared down the street, the taillights disappearing in the dark night. As Lisa approached the house the front door opened and a light was switched on, illuminating the small enclosed porch. A woman in her mid-forties stepped out. At first glance, she looked just like Debra, until a closer look revealed faint strands of silver in the dark hair and wrinkled lines around the eyes.

"Just in time for dinner." She held her arms out to Lisa.

"Mom." Lisa dropped her case to hug the older woman.

"You haven't been home in such a long time," Marianne Winters scolded her daughter lovingly, looking her up and down with a mother's critical stare. "You're also much too thin."

"I'm just fine," Lisa assured her.

Inside the house, her father, a tall man with graying, dark red hair enveloped her in a bear hug. "There's my girl." He kissed her soundly on the cheek, as she threw her arms around him.

"How's my favorite girl?" Bill asked fondly.

"Just fine."

"We can talk over dinner," Marianne interrupted, pushing them toward the dining room. "Everything is getting cold."

Lisa's eyes widened as she saw baked ham, mashed potatoes, green beans and applesauce, her favorite meal, covering the old-fashioned dining room table. "I can't eat all this," she protested.

"Oh, yes, you can," Marianne said firmly. "I doubt you take time for too many proper meals down there. You look much too thin for my piece of mind."

"She looks fine to me," Bill told his wife, as he took his place at the head of the table. "What I would like to know is why we weren't notified until after you were out of the hospital about your accident."

"Because I was all right," Lisa protested. "I just had some cuts and bruises."

"Debra mentioned that you were with your boss at the time and that he was badly hurt. How is he doing?" Marianne asked.

"Oh, Mr. Nolan doesn't believe in being kept down for too long." She lowered her lashes to hide the expression in her eyes.

"You've never said very much about him," her mother persisted. "Is he an easy man to work for? I believe he's younger than Mr. Connors." Disapproval of Mark was evident in her voice. Marianne had never been happy that Lisa was dating a man so much older than herself.

"He's thirty-two, a very hard-working and brilliant lawyer." Lisa pretended to concentrate on cutting her slice of ham to avoid looking up at her mother.

Over her downcast head, her parents exchanged a silent message.

The next day, an exhausted Lisa discovered how difficult it can be to find just the right wedding gown. She and Debra, along with their mothers, traipsed all over town, and by the time they had reached the sixth shop, Debra was almost in tears.

Please let this place have what she's looking for, Lisa silently pleaded.

And it did. When Debra tried on a white silk-and-lace gown, the agreement was unanimous. That was the gown meant for Debra, and she bought the sample, which hardly even needed to be altered. Lisa's gown, which they found in a local store that specialized in formal wear, was of a deep apricot silk, and she bought a matching silk flower for her hair.

"Well, that's out of the way," Marilyn Stevens, Debra's mother, sighed. When she stood next to Marianne, it was impossible for most people to tell them apart. That was how much the twin sisters still looked alike.

"Now, what about the invitations?" Marianne asked.

"Those I ordered earlier this week, and I can pick them up on Monday," Debra replied, suddenly looking very weary. "I don't know if I can stand looking at flowers today. Can the florist wait?"

The other three women agreed that their day had been full enough. It was time to go home and collapse.

That evening, while Lisa got ready for bed, her mother tapped on the door and peeked in. "Is it all right if I come in for a moment?" Marianne asked.

"Of course." Lisa smiled, curling up on her bed.

Marianne smiled back, seating herself on the end of the bed. She glanced at a photograph on the wall of Lisa and Debra in high school cheerleaders' outfits. "The two of you have come a long way since then. You've been inseparable since you were old enough to walk, much less talk. And now there are going to be a great many changes. So how are things with you, Lee? Mark is so much older than you are, but . . . well, how do you really feel about him?"

"He's a very nice man," Lisa said carefully. "I enjoy his company, but there's nothing serious between us."

"Please don't think that I'm trying to push you into marriage because of Debra," her mother assured her. "I've always been glad that you two never competed with each other in everything you did. I guess I'm just a little afraid that you'll get wedding fever and marry before you are ready, maybe to the wrong man."

"There's no fear of that happening," Lisa said quietly. It was difficult to imagine that anyone could stir her blood the same way that Dan did. And she knew she couldn't settle for anything less.

"Just don't wait so long that I'm too old to enjoy my grandchildren," Marianne chided lovingly, leaning forward to kiss her daughter's cheek. "Good night, dear."

Lisa lay awake a good part of the night, wondering what it would be like if she were planning her wedding instead of Debra's. The trouble was that the groom she always pictured turned out to have dark blond hair and glittering blue eyes! Punching her pillow angrily, she rolled over and went to sleep.

Back at the apartment one afternoon, Lisa started sorting through the wedding responses that they were receiving every day, checking the names off against the master list. Her hand trembled as she picked up one response that was written in a bold, familiar hand.

"Deb, you . . ." She spoke through stiff lips. "You never told me you had invited Dan."

"Oh, didn't I?" Debra was all innocence. "Isn't it nice that he accepted?"

"You barely know the man," Lisa persisted, twisting her clammy hands together. "Why did you do it?"

"Chalk it up to my impulsive nature." Debra left the room, an enigmatic smile curving her lips.

When the special day arrived, Debra stood before a large mirror while Lisa adjusted her veil. Even though Debra hadn't at first cared to have the large wedding her parents had always desired for her, she had thrown herself into the activities wholeheartedly, and she had ended up enjoying all of the fuss involved.

"I wish the butterflies would go away," Debra

groaned, pressing a hand against her stomach. She turned as a tall, gray-haired man entered the room.

"My beautiful daughter," John Stevens said quietly. "We have a gentleman waiting for you outside. Shall we join him?"

"I think so." Debra's voice trembled as she spoke.

Lisa's eyes shimmered with unshed tears as she stood next to Debra while the couple recited their vows. There was no question as to Pat's love for her cousin. His face had lit up when she had appeared at the end of the aisle in the small church.

Lisa had also seen Dan's tall figure out of the corner of her eye as she had walked down the aisle in front of Debra. Her stomach had fluttered as she realized that Morgan was not standing beside him. Her fears hadn't come true after all. He had come alone.

Lisa endured the picture-taking with impatience, anxious to find out if Dan would also attend the reception. Looking delicate and fragile in her apricot silk, she moved among the guests, looking for one special, tall figure. Finally spying him, she walked up and welcomed him with a smile.

"What a pleasant surprise, Dan." Lisa held her hands out in greeting, her face radiant. "The least you can do now is dance with me."

"The gentleman is supposed to ask the lady to dance," Dan pointed out with a smile to match hers.

"You never said you were a gentleman," Lisa said lightly. "And I never said I was a lady." She took him by the hand, leading him to the dance floor.

"Any old boyfriends here?" he asked.

"Dozens." She impishly wrinkled her nose. "Would you care to meet some of them?"

"Not really." Dan's voice seemed almost distant as he took her into his arms. He looked down at her smiling face. "Where's Connors? I'm surprised that he's letting you run around loose."

"He wasn't invited," Lisa replied firmly, looking up at him.

For a moment it seemed that Dan's arms tightened around her as he heard her reply. "You look beautiful today, Lee."

"Only the bride is supposed to look beautiful," she said breathlessly.

"I wasn't watching the bride." Dan pressed her closer against him.

After their dance, they moved over to one corner of the large room; Dan left her momentarily to fetch two glasses of champagne. Lisa saw her mother motion toward her.

"My parents would like to meet you," Lisa said demurely, when Dan returned with their champagne.

"Fine," he answered. "I'd like to meet them, too."

When she introduced Dan to her parents, Lisa noticed that her mother studied him carefully.

"Have dinner with us after the reception, Mr. Nolan," Marianne said graciously.

"Thank you; I'd like that." Dan smiled at her, his charm readily evident.

"Lisa can direct you to our home." Marianne said, simply assuming that Lisa would be staying with him for the remainder of the reception. "We'll see you around seven."

The time passed rapidly; soon Lisa was assisting Debra into her going-away suit and then she was joining the rest of the guests to wave the bride and groom off for their honeymoon.

Half an hour later, Lisa and Dan walked out to his car, with Lisa self-consciously holding the bridal bouquet. She had had no choice but to catch it; Debra seemed to have throw it directly at her. After she gave him the directions to her home, Dan switched on the engine. As he drove down the street Lisa leaned her head back against the seat, allowing herself to feel the weariness she had been staving off for the past two weeks.

"Hectic?" Dan asked quietly, shooting a quick glance at her profile.

"Very." She smiled. "Work is a breeze compared to these past few weeks."

All too soon, Dan parked his car in the driveway and got out, walking around to help Lisa out. "Where's your car?" He looked around with a puzzled frown.

"At home; I drove up with Deb. I thought I'd fly back tomorrow."

"If you don't mind leaving tonight, you can drive back with me," he offered.

"Thank you." Lisa led the way to the front door, her heart thudding. "I'd like that."

Lisa's mother was resting on the couch, her feet propped up on the coffee table, while her father was lazing in a large easy chair, reading the paper.

"You're just in time." Marianne greeted them with a weary smile. "The roast will be done in about twenty minutes."

"Then I think I'll go up and change first." Lisa headed for the stairs. When she came back down, casually dressed in tan denim pants and an old green cotton shirt she had discovered in a drawer, she saw that Dan had discarded his suit coat and tie. "I'll set the table, Mom," she offered.

Marianne followed her daughter into the kitchen, checking on the dinner as Lisa got out plates and silverware.

"I like him," her mother said honestly. "He's a man who's going to go far in his profession. The two of you make a striking couple."

"Oh, please don't say anything like that in front of him," Lisa begged. "He's let it be known that he values his freedom too much to give it up for anyone."

"That's what they all say." Marianne smiled. "And they usually fall the hardest when the time comes, too."

"Dan's offered to give me a lift home tonight," Lisa told her.

"You're going to be awfully tired," her mother warned her. "You've been up since dawn."

"I know, but I can sleep as late as I want tomorrow," Lisa assured her.

Lisa was secretly pleased that Dan and her father had discovered several mutual interests and that they were able to talk easily throughout the meal and afterwards as well, while she helped her mother wash the dishes.

After the dishes were finished, Lisa went upstairs to pack her suitcase, eager to be ready when Dan was. After an hour or so of casual conversation, Dan suggested they go, since they had a long drive ahead of them. Lisa's suitcase was stowed in the trunk of Dan's car as she hugged her parents good-bye, promising another visit soon.

"I'm glad to have met you, Dan." Marianne smiled. "I hope we see you again."

"Thank you for dinner." He grasped her proferred hand. "And don't worry; I'll get Lisa home safely."

"I'm sure you will."

Lisa got into the car as Dan switched on the ignition. As they drove down the street, he switched on the radio, selecting a station playing soft music. "If you'd like to take a nap, go ahead," he suggested. "It's going to be a long drive."

"That doesn't seem fair to you," Lisa protested.

"You look worn out, so go ahead. It won't bother me."

Lisa rested her head against the car seat and closed her eyes. The gentle motion of the car soon lulled her to sleep, and it wasn't long before her head dropped onto Dan's shoulder. He glanced down, smiling at her peaceful features. He shifted his arm to encircle her shoulders, pulling her closer to him.

"Lisa." A soft, insistent voice penetrated her dreamworld. She wrinkled her nose, murmuring unintelligibly. "Lisa, you're home," the soft voice persisted.

Lisa became hazily aware that a steady warmth was surrounding her and that her cheek was resting against a firm surface. She opened her eyes and discovered that her head was on Dan's shoulder and that his arm was around her.

"I'm sorry," she apologized, starting to sit up, pushing her hair away from her eyes. "I'm afraid I wasn't very good company for you."

"You were fine," Dan told her.

"Would you like to come in for some coffee?"

"No, thanks; it's pretty late." He got out of the car and walked around to open her door. After getting her suitcase out of the trunk, Dan walked her to her apartment.

"Thank you for the ride." Lisa looked up with a warm smile.

"My pleasure." He took the key out of her hand and inserted it into the lock. Dan pushed the door open and carried Lisa's suitcase inside. She followed him, aware of how empty the apartment seemed with Debra gone. Dan stared down at her face, watching the various emotions cross her features.

"You can be sure I'll be in the office bright and early on Monday," Lisa said, looking up at Dan. The words faded as she saw the expression on his face.

"Who says the bride should get all the kisses?" Dan growled, pulling her into his arms. His kiss was explosive. Lisa clutched his shoulders, afraid that her trembling legs wouldn't support her. He took his time with her, demanding a response from her that she was unable to refuse. A soft moan escaped her lips when Dan finally lifted his head. His breathing was as ragged as hers.

"Dan," Lisa whispered, lifting her hand to caress his cheek.

"You couldn't respond to me the way you just did if you felt anything at all for Connors," he muttered thickly against her hair. "He doesn't really mean anything to you, does he?"

"Would it matter?" she asked provocatively.

"Please just answer me." Dan's grip was merciless. There would be bruises left on her skin in the morning.

"Mark doesn't mean anything to me." Lisa looked up at his dark face with glowing eyes.

"We need to do some talking, then," Dan told her. "But not now, because the last thing I want to do right now is talk. I'll be over tomorrow night with a pizza at six. Just do me a favor and don't wear anything too sexy. I don't know if my blood pressure could handle it."

Lisa smiled at Dan's arrogant assumption that she would fall so readily in with his plans. But all she cared about right now was that she was in his arms, and she didn't want him to leave.

"Oh, Lee, I don't want to leave you," he groaned, pulling her against him for another hard kiss. A moment later, however, the front door closed behind him.

Lisa stood still, touching her swollen lips with her fingertips. A slow smile lit up her face. In a dream-like trance she walked into the bedroom and got ready for bed.

Welcoming the luxury of being able to laze the day away, Lisa slept late the next day, and she spent the afternoon washing her hair and manicuring her nails, polishing them with a pale-rose shade.

Wearing a muted blue-silk caftan with a plunging neckline that clung to her body as she walked, and leaving her hair in a loose, curly style, Lisa knew she was ready for Dan. Hearing the doorbell, she hurried to answer it.

"Hi," Dan said huskily, setting the pizza carton down on a table and drawing her into his arms. "Um, I've been waiting for this all day," he murmured against her lips.

"Me too." Her voice was a hoarse whisper as she linked her arms around his neck.

"I think we'd better eat before I get any more ideas," Dan said, reluctantly pulling her away from him.

"I'll get some plates." Lisa walked into the kitchen, the silken folds of her caftan flowing about her ankles.

During the meal, Dan kept things casual with light, teasing comments. Once, when his eyes met hers in an intense gaze, Lisa felt as if she were caught in a web. Heat rose in her body before she could turn her eyes away from his.

When they finished eating, Lisa carried the dishes into the kitchen, stacking them into the dishwasher. She could hear Dan putting records on the record player, the soft strains drifting through the air. When she came back into the living room, Dan smiled at her, as he pulled her over to a nearby chair, cradling her in his lap.

"You taste delicious, smell delicious," he murmured, nuzzling her neck.

"You said we were going to talk," Lisa reminded him, twisting her head away from him.

"You don't make it easy do you?" Dan groaned, his hands sliding down to her waist. "Okay, we'll talk, then. I want some answers."

"Answers?" she asked curiously.

"Yes. Like why didn't you come to see me more often when I was in the hospital? Why did you suddenly withdraw? Why did you decide to run back into Connors' arms?" Dan paused for a minute. "Especially after that Sunday afternoon. I thought—gosh, I don't know what I thought." He raked his fingers wearily through his hair.

"I know what *I* thought," Lisa said softly, still feeling the remembered pain. "You didn't want to jeopardize your affair with Morgan Grant. She appears to be very possessive where you are concerned."

"Honey, making love to Morgan would be like making love to a deep freeze," Dan told her, his fingers caressing the soft skin of her throat. "Now, as for you . . ." His fingers continued to ply her soft, silky skin. "You're warm, passionate, loving," he murmured. "You're all that any man could desire. Was that really the reason why you didn't come?"

"Yes," she replied in a choked voice.

"When I called you the day I was released from the hospital, and when you had the guts to coolly inform me that you had a date, I wanted to strangle you," Dan growled. "Then, later, you showed up at my door drunk, chattering away like some crazy magpie."

"I felt so foolish afterwards," Lisa confessed, pressing her lips against his throat, delighting in the rapid beat of his pulse, knowing she was the cause.

"Is that why you didn't want me to touch you that night?" His lips followed the path of his hands, as they teased the sensitive skin of her breasts.

"I—I . . ." She found it hard to think coherently. "I didn't want you to kiss me and pretend that I was Morgan instead."

Dan swore softly under his breath. "There's no way that I would want you to be Morgan. I could easily tell the two of you apart in the dark. You're the warm and soft one." His lips traveled upward to recapture hers, first teasing them with a feathery touch, then his tongue outlined her mouth. Moaning softly, Lisa tugged at his hair, bringing his lips fully down on her parted ones, wanting all that he could give her. The buttons of his shirt parted as her hands slipped inside, wrapping themselves around his waist, moving over his bare back. When Dan's lips finally left hers, Lisa's head was spinning, as if she had had too much to drink. She rested her cheek against his bare chest, aware of the heavy thud of his heartbeat.

"If you don't like Morgan very much, why do you always date her? And why did you take her to the picnic?" Lisa asked in a small voice.

"Because I knew you'd be there with over-the-hill Connors. Hey!" he yelled as she playfully punched him. "I wanted to see if I could get a rise out of you." Dan grinned wickedly. "And I did."

"That still doesn't tell me why you date her."

Dan took a deep breath. "You might say she's a shield for me."

"I can't see you hiding behind any woman," she teased lightly.

Dan gently pushed Lisa away and stood up. He raked agitated fingers through his hair, keeping his back to her.

"Morgan's in love with you, Dan," Lisa continued softly. "And she intends to be Mrs. Dan Nolan."

"Morgan knew the score from the beginning," he said grimly. "So did every other woman I dated. They knew not to expect any long-term commitment. I don't ever plan to go through the same agony my father did."

Lisa's blood ran cold at the bitterness in Dan's voice. "You've never said very much about your family."

"What is there to say?" His mouth twisted cruelly, as he turned back to face her. "My mother decided that she couldn't be happy with just one man, but she enjoyed the security of marriage too much to give it up. As my father had to travel a great deal, she could play around all she wanted to and still act the part of the happy housewife when he was home. I found out about her extracurricular activities when I was ten. People didn't seem to care that you might overhear them, even when they were talking about your own family. We lived in a small town and my mother was the greatest subject of gossip that the old biddies had. From that experience, I determined that a woman would never hurt me like she had done to my father. He must have known what was going on, but he never said a word. He loved her no matter how much she dragged his name through the mud."

"Not all women are like that, Dan." Lisa felt sorry for the small boy who had hardened his heart so early in life. "You can't blame all women because of one. Many women are happy to share their lives with just one man. Unfortunately, your mother felt she needed to find her happiness outside of the home. You shouldn't hate her. If anything, you should pity her."

"You're too emotional for your own good, Lee," Dan said harshly. "That's why you're hurt so easily. I hated thinking that you had fallen in love with Connors, only to get hurt. And I didn't want to hurt you, either."

"Why, Dan?" she asked.

"I don't know," he said slowly. "Maybe because you seemed too good to be true. You didn't seem real."

Lisa ran over to him, slipped her arms around his waist and pressed herself against him. She knew that, whether he cared to say it or not, Dan was beginning to feel the emotions he had been burying for so long. It would take a long time to peel away those layers of armor, but she didn't care. "I'm very real," she said huskily. She knew she had to go carefully to preserve the fragile threads of their relationship. "Mark was my defense against you. I thought you wanted Morgan, and I was so afraid you'd see how much I enjoyed being with you. And I didn't want to let you hurt me."

Dan's arms went around her, tightening with the intensity of his feelings. "You need someone more lasting than me, Lee." He buried his face against her hair, inhaling the soft scent of her fragrant hair. "Someone who can give you a feeling of permanence."

She closed her eyes, wildly wishing she could tell him how much she loved him. But that was the last thing Dan would want to hear. He didn't want any woman to love him, just as he didn't want to fall in love. She could only take it slowly, a step at a time.

"If you could learn to have more trust in me—she took great care in choosing her words—"then you would soon see that all women aren't as bad as you think they are. I could be sort of a guinea pig for you."

"You're not at all like the guinea pigs I had as a boy." His smile softened his harsh features. "You're definitely more desirable."

"Would you be willing to give it a try?" Lisa looked up, still keeping her arms around him.

"I've never told anyone about my mother before," he mused, resting his chin on the top of her head, not answering her.

"Then it's a good thing you finally opened up and confided it," Lisa told him.

Dan tipped her chin up, studying her face for long

moments. "Perhaps I did it because I had a sincere listener," he said quietly. "Thank you."

"Any time," she whispered, afraid to break the fragile spell surrounding them.

"I should be going," Dan said. Keeping his arm around her, he walked toward the front door. "I'll see you in the morning." He brushed a light kiss across her lips before leaving.

Chapter Nine

As the days passed, subtle changes between Lisa and her boss were occurring in the office. Although their business-like treatment of each other was outwardly just as formal as before, there were slight differences, as in the way Dan's eyes seemed warmer than usual when they lingered on his secretary, or in the huskier tone of Lisa's voice when she spoke to him.

One morning, Lisa had been busier than usual preparing Dan's presentation for a court case he had that day. But a smile lingered on her lips as she remembered Dan's remarks when he had finished his dictation earlier.

"Miss Winters," his voice was deceptively soft, while

his eyes danced with wicked lights, "if just one more button slips open on that dress of yours before the end of the day, you better be prepared to be attacked on the spot."

"I'll keep that in mind, Mr. Nolan," Lisa said primly, although lights also danced in her eyes.

She had just finished proofreading her typing when someone approached her desk. With a sinking heart, Lisa looked up to see Morgan's cool features.

"Good morning, Miss Winters," the blonde said silkily. "I'd like to see Dan, please."

"Certainly," Lisa murmured, punching the intercom button. "Mr. Nolan, Miss Grant is here."

"Drat," he breathed softly. "Send her in."

"Go on in," Lisa said coolly.

"Darling, I was just in seeing Uncle, and I thought you could save my life by taking me to lunch," Morgan said throatily, as she closed the door behind her.

Lisa clasped her hands in front of her, wishing the angry trembling in her stomach would go away. It wasn't Dan's fault that Morgan had showed up, so why did she feel so angry toward him?

Five minutes later, the inner office door opened and Morgan walked out, with Dan following.

"I'll be back around one-thirty, Miss Winters," he told Lisa in a formal voice. She merely nodded, not trusting her own voice.

With her own appetite gone, Lisa spent her lunch hour wandering through the various stores in the area. Her overactive imagination ran rampant. What had been Morgan's real reason for suddenly showing up at the office? And who was Uncle?

Her questions were answered when she picked up the telephone messages from the receptionist on her way back to work.

"I've found out something about that sexy blonde who's always coming in to see Mr. Nolan!" Tina said in an eager whisper, as Lisa stood glancing rapidly through the messages, mentally deciding which were the most important. "I hadn't know she was Mr. Patterson's niece!"

"Niece?" Lisa looked up in surprise.

"Now I understand why she's always acted so self-important around here," Tina went on. "I bet she was even the one who persuaded Nr. Nolan to join the firm."

"Possibly," Lisa murmured. Now she understood why Morgan acted so possessive toward Dan. The news did not make her feel any better.

Lisa was still pondering over this new information when Dan returned from lunch. "Did you have a nice lunch?" she asked frostily.

"It's a pity I didn't get indigestion, isn't it?" Dan grinned at her as he walked into his own office.

Refusing to rise to the bait, Lisa merely called him uncomplimentary names under her breath as she returned to her work. Her cool silence continued for the remainder of the afternoon, but it had no effect on Dan's cheerful mood. The moment the clock reached quitting time, she hastily covered her typewriter and reached for her purse.

"What now?" she muttered as the intercom line buzzed. In a formal voice, she said, "Yes, sir?"

"Would you come in here, please?" he asked crisply.

Grimacing, Lisa got up and walked into the inner office. Dan was seated at a work table he had set up on the other side of the large office.

"Close the door, please," Dan ordered, not looking up from his work. Mystified, Lisa obeyed. Dan turned in his chair to face her. The expression on his face was unreadable. "Come here," he said softly.

"Did you need one of the files?" she asked, walking toward the table. When she was close enough, Dan reached out, pulling her toward him, keeping a firm grip on her wrists.

"In a better mood now?" he asked, pulling her even closer.

"No."

"Maybe I can improve it." Dan stood up, their bodies lightly touching. Before his hand could reach the nape of her neck, she had smoothly glided away toward the window.

"I doubt it." Lisa said, looking out the window. She was determined not to let Dan have his way. At least, not too easily.

Dan leaned against a corner of the table, watching Lisa with amusement, as if he knew her intent. "Please come here." His words were softly spoken.

Lisa took her time turning around and walking slowly toward him. His arms slid around her waist, pressing her against him.

"Dan, not here!" Lisa protested, putting her hands against his chest to prevent the embrace. "What if someone should come in?"

"Everyone knows that if my door is closed it is *not* advisable to enter," he murmured, jerking her off balance so that she fell against him. Dan's mouth closed over hers in that sweet searing way she knew so well.

Lisa's hands slid up over Dan's shoulders. "This is crazy," she said softly.

"That is all your fault," he said huskily, recapturing her lips.

"Dan, I—" The couple turned in surprise at the intrusion, Dan's face dark with anger and Lisa's still bemused from his kisses. Morgan Grant stood in the doorway, her icy eyes taking in the embracing couple.

Flushing hotly, Lisa tried to pull away, but Dan's arms tightened, preventing her. "My closed door means that I don't care to be disturbed, Morgan," he said coldly.

"So I see." The blonde woman's eyes were merciless as they raked over Lisa. "I noticed that your light was on. I assumed that your *secretary* had left for the day. I thought we could have dinner together." Her voice turned harsh when she turned to Lisa. "I see you didn't take my advice, Miss Winters."

Dan silently surveyed Morgan. "You'd better go home, Lisa," he said quietly, letting his arms drop to his sides.

"Dan, I . . ." She felt a growing dismay.

"Go home," he said flatly, his eyes still on Morgan.

Not wishing to show how hurt she felt in front of Morgan, Lisa quickly left the room under Morgan's triumphant gaze. Lisa held her tears back until she reached the apartment. In her bedroom, she shed her clothes quickly, uncharacteristically dropping them in an untidy heap, and she pulled on a short robe. She flopped down on her bed, dissolving into tears. She felt numb after Dan's earlier actions. She couldn't bear the thought of going in to work the next day and facing him.

She was still lying on the bed, steeped in self-pity, when the doorbell rang much later. Burying her head in her pillow, she tried to ignore the insistent ringing. Finally, realizing that it wasn't going to end, she got off her bed and walked into the living room. Opening the door, her face hardened when she saw Dan. He anticipated her move, swiftly moving to block her attempt to close the door on him.

"Don't shut me out, Lee," Dan said quietly, moving quickly past her.

"Get out," she choked, keeping the door open. "I don't want to talk to you, Dan. Go back to Morgan. You've made your choice; that was only too clear today in your office. I guess it's because her uncle is one of the senior partners, and I'm sure the match will be very beneficial to your career."

Dan let out a deep breath, swearing softly. He jerked the door out of her hand, slamming it shut. Then he gripped her wrist and pulled her over to the sofa, pushing her down on the cushions. He quickly sat down too, keeping hold of her arms to prevent her from moving away. Her green eyes shot angry sparks at him.

"Why can't you just leave me alone?" Her voice was a tortured whisper. "Wasn't my humiliation enough?"

"I wasn't trying to humiliate you, Lee," Dan said gently. "I just wanted you out of there before I had my talk with Morgan. I wanted to tell Morgan exactly what

I thought of her, and I didn't want you to hear that kind of language," he said wryly.

Lisa looked at him with confusion. "I—I don't understand."

"I didn't appreciate her high-handed attitude, just coming into my office like that. Then, after I told you to go home, she began feeling pretty sure of herself where I was concerned," Dan said quietly. "I don't know exactly what she has said to you, but I have an idea. Morgan knows now to stay out of my life. She even tried to make empty threats about talking to her uncle and ruining my career. But he's too smart a man for that."

Tears began streaming down Lisa's cheeks. "When you told me to leave tonight, I just wanted to die."

Groaning, Dan gathered her into his arms, pressing her face against his shirt front. "I hated myself for putting that hurt look on your face. But I knew I had to have you out of there before I lit into Morgan. I didn't want you involved in any more ugliness." He stroked her hair in a comforting gesture.

Relieved that she hadn't lost Dan after all, Lisa began crying again. All her pent-up tension escaped as Dan kept his arms around her, soothing her as he rubbed his cheek against her hair. When her sobs finally began to subside, she took several deep breaths, searching for control.

"I look horrible," Lisa said finally, adding, "And I got your shirt soaking wet!"

"It won't hurt it," he said quietly, his hand against her cheek, his thumbs sensually massaging the soft skin behind her ears. His slow smile was enough to melt her. "I don't give a hang about my shirt." He said each word slowly, to allow it to sink in. "All I want is for you to stop crying so I can kiss you."

Smiling back, she happily complied.

Lisa's days soon settled into a comfortable pattern. She and Dan would either dine out one or two times a week, or Lisa would fix them a meal at her apartment.

One Friday evening, they attended a play, but Lisa found it difficult to pay attention while Dan, lifting her palm to his lips, let his tongue run over her hand. Each time she tried to retrieve her hand he would tighten his grip, making it difficult for her to struggle.

"You did that deliberately," she accused him as they walked outside to his car after the play.

"What?" he asked innocently.

"You know very well what." Lisa could feel a flush rise in her cheeks.

"I didn't like that play much," Dan commented, as he unlocked the passenger door for Lisa.

"Who could concentrate when . . ." Lisa stopped, seeing the wicked grin on Dan's face as he slid behind the wheel. "Oh, Dan." She laughed huskily, shaking her head in amusement. "You're terrible."

Dan's hand hesitated on the ignition key. He half turned to face her. One hand lifted, the knuckles lightly brushing her cheek. "Lee, come home with me," he murmured, looking deep into her eyes.

Lisa's breath caught in her throat. Dan's meaning was all too clear. And all too tempting. She was well aware of the effect Dan's touch had on her—and the effect hers had on him. Dan would be an excellent lover, she had no doubt of that. But she wanted more than physical love from him, and she didn't know if she would ever be able to get it.

Seeing her hesitation, he leaned over, teasing a corner of her lips. "You wouldn't need to be afraid with me." His warm breath fanned her cheek.

"Dan, I . . ." Her voice drifted off. Her body was ready to say yes, while her mind screamed no. "I . . . I can't."

"Can't?" he murmured sensuously against her skin. "I'll even serve you breakfast in bed."

Lisa's hands moved upward, and she let her fingers comb through his thick hair. She gave herself up to his kiss, and she was trembling when he finally released her.

"Changed your mind?" Dan asked huskily against her lips.

"I have always subscribed to an unwritten rule that I will never sleep with my boss," she whispered.

"She's not only beautiful but she also has ethics." He smiled as he turned to switch on the car, not seeming surprised by her answer.

Lisa leaned back, feeling irritated that Dan could be so calm while her own emotions were in such turmoil!

Dan pulled into the apartment parking lot and switched off the engine. Then he got out of the car and helped Lisa out. At her door, he pulled her into his arms and kissed her thoroughly. Her mouth parted under his, letting his kiss deepen. Lisa's blood raced under his sensual touch. When he finally let her go, his breathing was uneven. "Good night, Lisa."

Wide-eyed, she watched him turn to leave. "Dan, I—" Lisa's hand lifted. She suddenly didn't want him to leave without her.

He turned and smiled. "Go to bed, Lisa," Dan said softly. "Alone—before we both change our minds again."

Lisa walked into the darkened apartment, feeling bereft. Later, crawling into bed, she lay back, recalling those moments in Dan's arms. If she hadn't been so cowardly she would still be in his arms right now. A feeling of longing spread through her body. It was past dawn before she finally fell asleep.

The next few weeks were hectic and tiring for Lisa. It was all she could do to drag herself home to flop into bed each evening.

One morning began all wrong when her alarm didn't go off. She overslept and had to rush to get ready for work. By the time she reached the office, she had a pounding headache.

"Keeping late hours, Miss Winters?" Dan asked sarcastically when Lisa sat at her desk.

"Not lately," she snapped, wishing he would go away and let her suffer in peace.

"Complaining?" His voice was softly taunting.

"Look, I've got a pounding headache and "

"You're not supposed to admit to those until after you're married, Miss Winters," Dan said over his shoulder as he walked away.

Lisa gritted her teeth, refusing the temptation to throw something at Dan's broad back. She knew that Dan had been snappish because of a crucial upcoming court case, the outcome of which was very important to him. As usual, he had been working in his office long after she would have left for the day, and he would already be there in the morning when she arrived.

Lisa was herself too tired to worry about Dan's own overtaxing schedule.

"Would it be possible for you to come in for a few hours tomorrow?" Dan asked one Friday afternoon. "Ordinarily I wouldn't ask but, as you know, I have to sum up on Monday."

"Of course I'll come in." Lisa was surprised by the hesitancy in Dan's voice. "You thought I'd refuse, didn't you?"

"I wouldn't have blamed you," he wryly replied. "I admit I haven't been the most congenial boss the past couple of weeks. I'm surprised I haven't gotten a cup of coffee in my lap."

"Don't give me any ideas," she said sweetly. "I'll be in at nine."

"Fine."

The next day Lisa saw no reason to wear a dress, opting instead for jeans and a blue cotton shirt. Dan dressed casually, too. Lisa found the typing to be done already on her desk so, without a word, she sat down and began working.

Like a carefully tooled machine, the two worked together in silence, until a stack of papers piled on Dan's desk was proof that the job was done.

"I really appreciate this." Dan smiled gratefully at Lisa. "Come on, I'll buy you a late lunch." He didn't give her time to refuse.

At a nearby coffee shop, Lisa could see the lines of strain gradually disappear from Dan's face.

"I know I haven't been the most amiable of people lately." Dan picked up her hand, idly playing with her fingers. "Am I forgiven?"

"You know you are," Lisa said softly, letting her eyes meet his intent gaze.

"Lisa!" Startled, she looked up to find Mark coming swiftly toward her.

"Mark." At her breathless voice, Dan's eyes narrowed. Lisa was uneasily aware of his studied gaze on her flushed face.

A curious expression came into Mark's eyes as he focused on Lisa's companion.

"We worked in the office today," Lisa nervously explained, angry with herself for her faltering voice.

"How about having dinner with me tonight?" Mark asked her, ignoring Dan completely. "I haven't seen you for weeks."

"Lisa is busy tonight and any other night," Dan curtly interrupted, rising quickly. "Time to go home, Lee." His voice was an intimate caress that couldn't be misunderstood.

Lisa looked up with snapping eyes, and a flush rose to her cheeks. Mark looked back and forth between the two with a puzzled expression. Then comprehension slowly dawned. "Oh, I see," he said slowly.

"No, you don't see," Lisa said angrily, keeping her eyes on Dan.

"Yes, I do." Mark smiled at her with understanding in his eyes. "Good-bye, Lee. I wish you luck."

"What makes you think you can—" Lisa turned angrily to Dan after they got outside. She took several deep breaths to control her rapidly rising temper. "How could you do such a terrible thing?"

"It was easy," Dan replied tautly.

Lisa sputtered uselessly as Dan practically dragged

her toward his Buick. He pushed her inside and walked around to the driver's side.

"Don't you realize what you let Mark think about us?" she demanded, half-turning in her seat. "He–he thinks we're—" she stopped, unable to continue.

"Living together," Dan mockingly finished for her. "At least he won't take a chance and call you at home. Now he'll think that I might answer the phone."

"That's disgusting," Lisa said hotly.

"He certainly looked happy to see you," he said harshly. "You've walked all over that guy and he still has you on a pedestal."

"And what's wrong with that? I think it's very sweet. *He* knows how to treat a lady." Lisa sat back in her seat with a defiant toss of her head.

Swearing under his breath, Dan turned the car down a quiet side street and turned off the engine. "Good for him," he said sarcastically. "But I know how to treat a *woman*." Dan gripped Lisa's shoulders and pulled her toward him. She twisted her face away, but Dan's hand took her chin in a bruising grip. "He's too nice and soft-hearted for you," he muttered thickly against her lips. "You snap your fingers and he jumps. Well, lady, you need someone who's more stubborn than you. Who won't put up with it."

Lisa kept her mouth closed, refusing to yield to Dan's mastery. Her eyes remained defiantly open, shooting emerald sparks at his hard, chiseled features. When he finally lifted his head her face was a frozen mask. "Take me home," Lisa said coldly.

"With pleasure," Dan snarled, turning back to switch the ignition on.

Lisa sat back; she had never felt as angry as she did

right then at Dan. When he stopped the car in front of her apartment house, Lisa hastily jerked the door open and scrambled out. Just as she began to slam the door shut a thought occurred to her. "My car!" Lisa cried out. "My car is still at the office."

"Then you know it's safe, don't you?" Dan said mockingly, as he pressed his foot on the accelerator. The car roared off, the tires squealing on the asphalt.

Lisa watched him go, incredulous. She clenched her fists at her sides, muttering under her breath. She couldn't at that moment think of a fate horrible enough for Dan Nolan.

Chapter Ten

Lisa was glad on Monday that Dan would not be in the office. Smiling to herself, she efficiently dealt with any problems that cropped up. The only word she had from Dan was a brief telephone message in which he said that the judge's decision, handed down late that afternoon, had been in his client's favor. He obviously had not forgotten the events of the weekend, either.

The following morning, Lisa put her plan into effect. She first called the office and, deliberately coughing into the phone, told the receptionist she would not be in that day. Then she replaced the receiver and went back to bed.

An hour later, when the telephone rang, Lisa knew it was Dan.

"Hello." She made sure her voice sounded husky.

"Blast you, you're not sick." Dan's harsh voice was accusing.

"I have some kind of virus, so I have an idea I'll be out for a few days," Lisa lied glibly. Dan replied with several mildly profane remarks concerning her virus. "I'm afraid I have to hang up now; my head is spinning around and around." She said this faintly, then replaced the receiver.

It wasn't long before the phone began ringing again. Ignoring the persistent sound, Lisa turned over, pulling her pillow over her ears. She was surprised that she could fall back asleep so easily. During the rest of the day the telephone rang insistently several times but, knowing it was Dan, Lisa refused to answer it. She waited until the next day.

"As for your illness," Dan growled into the phone, "I want you to bring in a doctor's note when you decide to come back to work." On that note, he slammed the receiver down in her ear.

"A doctor's note he'll get," Lisa murmured to herself, as she quickly dialed a number.

Lisa stayed home for three days. After Dan's call demanding a doctor's note, he did not call again. Her face was composed when, returning to work, she walked into Dan's office.

"I'm glad to see that you finally decided to 'get well,'" he said sarcastically.

"Here's the doctor's note you requested," Lisa murmured, handing Dan a folded piece of paper.

He opened the paper, scanning the scrawled words. "I said a note from your doctor, *not* from your father." Dan looked up with hard eyes.

"My father *is* a doctor," she quietly pointed out. "In case you didn't notice, it's written on his office stationery."

"He is also an obstetrician," Dan countered.

"You didn't specify the kind of doctor," she said innocently. "And besides, even though my father has never performed any type of surgery on me because of the medical code of ethics, he *has* treated me for minor illnesses. He's really the only doctor I have."

Heaving an exasperated sigh, Dan crushed the note and tossed it into the wastebasket. "You've made your point," he said bleakly. "Now, just get out of here before I lose my temper."

Lisa mentally chalked up a point for her side as she left Dan's office. She felt very pleased with herself. The days she had spent at home hadn't been wasted. She had filled them by thinking over her feelings for Dan—and his for her. The idea that he might have been jealous of Mark occurred to her, and it pleased her. Secure in her thoughts, Lisa remained impervious to Dan's sarcasm for the balance of the week, smiling sweetly at him whenever he tried to be abusive.

"Don't patronize me," Dan growled one afternoon as she laid some papers on his desk to be signed.

"I'm sorry if you feel I'm patronizing you, Mr. Nolan," she said demurely as she left his office, his angry mutterings in her ears.

Lisa left work Friday evening intending to visit her parents for the weekend. She needed to be away from home and away from a phone that didn't ring any longer. The silence was becoming more than she could bear.

Lisa enjoyed a quiet weekend working with her

father in his garden, helping him tend his roses, and she also helped her mother with her weekly baking. Marianne Winters believed in making her own bread, and it was a weekly task.

Marianne divided up the dough, placing each section in a pan, ready for baking. "How are you and Dan getting along?" she asked casually, sliding the pans into the hot oven.

"Fine." Lisa's tone matched her mother's. Her movements were purely mechanical as she mixed the ingredients for a coffee cake. "Except that I'm in love with Dan Nolan," she said quietly.

"And?"

"He doesn't believe in love or lasting relationships," Lisa said bleakly. She went on to relate the substance of Dan's talk with her about his mother and to share some of their subsequent fights. She ended by telling of the argument following the meeting with Mark at the coffee shop, and of how she retaliated by pretending to be sick.

"It seems like Dan's hooked on you and just doesn't realize it," Marianne commented. "He can't understand the feelings he has for you, so he hides them the only way he knows how—under a layer of indifference and arrogance."

"If that's the only way he can show his love, then I don't think I want any part of it any longer," Lisa said in a choked voice.

"I think you do. You'll just have to bide your time the same way he is. Continue to be patient with him, Lisa," her mother advised. "Show him that you're not at all like his mother. You could be rewarded in the end."

Lisa's talk with her mother gave her some confidence. But she still felt more than a little unsure of Dan when she entered the office Monday morning.

"Good morning. How was your weekend?" Dan asked her as she sat down at her desk.

"I spent it at my parents'." Her head was bent down as she put away her purse, so she didn't see the subtle relaxation of Dan's features.

"Lee," he began hesitantly, "I'll be honest. I've never apologized to a woman before, so this is very hard for me. If possible, could we try again?"

Lisa felt her pulse quicken, but she kept her face composed. "I don't see why not," she said casually.

"Dinner Friday night?"

"Fine."

Lisa and Dan were soon back to their former relationship. Except for one thing: Lisa was puzzled by Dan's new treatment of her when they were alone. He limited himself to holding her hand or to placing a casual arm around her shoulders. Any kisses were equally casual and fell mainly on her cheek, or, if on her lips, they were light pecks. He seemed to act more like an older brother or an old friend than a date.

"Sometimes I wonder if I've developed some horrible disfigurement," Lisa grumbled to herself one evening after Dan had left her apartment. They had gone out to a movie and dinner. Lisa had deliberately chosen a romantic love story, hoping it would give Dan a few ideas, but they shared no mind-shattering kisses or sensual caresses when they were finally alone.

One Friday afternoon, Lisa was busily typing a report for Dan when Mark stopped by her desk.

"You seem to be a very busy lady." He smiled down at her.

"I've become very good at pretending to be." Lisa's face sobered. "Mark, about that day in the coffee shop, I—"

Opening his mouth to answer, Mark looked up as Dan appeared in the doorway of his office. The latter's blue eyes narrowed on seeing Mark.

"Did you want to see me, Connors?" Dan asked crisply.

"No, I didn't," Mark replied, deliberately keeping his eyes on Lisa's face. "I'll call you this weekend, Lee."

After Mark left them, Dan turned to Lisa. "He can't keep away from you, can he?" he asked harshly.

Lisa replied in anger. "*You* of all people should know better," she said hotly. "You should also remember that I don't appreciate bringing up personalities in the office."

"Right." Dan walked back into his office, pointedly closing the door behind him.

Glad when it was past five o'clock, Lisa hurriedly picked up her purse and prepared to leave. At that moment, she wanted only to be far away from Dan. As she walked across the parking lot, her heels clicked on the concrete. She gasped as a figure stepped from the shadow of the building. Then she saw that it was Mark.

"Oh, Mark, you frightened me." Her hand against her throat was trembling.

"I'm sorry if I frightened you, Lee. I'd like to talk to you for a moment, though," he said quietly.

"Right now?" She looked surprised, as she looked

around the deserted parking lot. "Couldn't it wait until Monday?"

"I'm resigning from the firm on Monday," Mark said directly.

"But . . . but why?" Lisa was shocked by his pronouncement.

"I was made an offer I can't refuse." He named a large, well-known firm. "In fact, I'd like you to come with me as my secretary. I can promise you a substantial increase in salary."

"That's very flattering, Mark, but no, thank you. I'm very happy here."

"It's because of Nolan, isn't it?"

"Of course not," she quickly denied.

"It won't work, Lee. I've seen the way you look at him. And the way he acts so possessively toward you. But that only extends to you as his secretary, no more. Unless, of course, you're having an affair with him."

"You should know better, Mark," Lisa said angrily.

"I'm sorry," he said quietly. "I don't want you angry at me. I hope we can part as friends."

"We'll always be friends." Lisa touched his arm.

"Are friends allowed a parting kiss?" Mark asked her wistfully.

Lisa smiled, lifting her face. She was unprepared for his hungry kiss, but she could feel none of the stirrings she felt under Dan's touch.

"Good-bye, Lisa." Mark abruptly released her and walked away.

She stood watching his retreating figure with a feeling of sorrow, sorrow for the emotions she couldn't feel.

When Lisa reached home she felt ready to drop from fatigue. After a quick shower, she slipped on a yellow terry cloth wraparound robe. Pouring herself a glass of wine, she turned on the stereo and, humming to herself, walked into her bedroom. She curled up on her bed with a book, but concentration was difficult to achieve. While she was reading one page for the third time, the doorbell rang, disturbing her peace. Wondering who could be calling on her at this time, Lisa padded barefoot to the door, first looking through the peephole. Surprised to see Dan's tall figure outside, she hurriedly opened the door.

"Dan, what a surp—" Her greeting was cut off as he pushed past her.

"All alone?" Dan glanced around the room.

"I'm not exactly dressed for company," Lisa pointed out.

Dan crossed his arms in front of him, studying Lisa from head to foot in an insolent manner. "There are plenty of men who'd appreciate such a delectable picture."

Lisa defensively wrapped her robe more closely about her, aware that she wore nothing underneath. Dan was acting like a stranger. "Why are you here?"

Dan walked slowly toward her, and she backed away. She stiffened as she reached her closed bedroom door. He leaned forward, resting his hands against the wood on either side of her. "Do I need a reason?" he said. Whiskey fumes fanned her face.

"You're drunk," Lisa said flatly, feeling her stomach churn at his tone.

"I only wish I were." Dan's eyes were focused on her mouth. "Instead, I sat in a bar trying to get drunk. And trying to figure you out."

"Oh?" She pretended an indifference she didn't feel.

"Lady, you take the cake. You really do." Dan shook his head in disbelief. "Take your so-called virginal protests. The way you lead me down the garden path only so far, then turn on the virgin act so I feel guilty enough to draw back."

"I never did that," Lisa said coldly. "You've been the one who's been so correct and proper these past few weeks."

"I bet Mark Connors doesn't have to put up with your Little-Miss-Innocent act." Dan bent his face down close to hers.

In a pure reflex action, happening before Lisa herself even realized it, her hand shot out, making sharp contact with Dan's cheek. The muscles around his mouth tightened, and his eyes narrowed to angry slits. Lisa looked at him in surprised silence, her hand pressed against her mouth.

"You little—" Dan jerked roughly against her. His kiss was meant to be punishing; he didn't give her time to breathe.

"Please, Dan," Lisa pleaded, tearing her mouth away from his.

"Please, Dan," he mocked her, stooping to pick her up in his arms and carry her into the darkened bedroom. Without ceremony, Dan dropped her onto the bed and proceeded to unbutton his shirt, pulling it free from his pants.

Lisa sat up, wide-eyed. "What are you doing?" she asked hoarsely, dreading his answer.

"Getting ready for bed," he said with a deadly calm. "What's wrong? Doesn't Connors take his shirt off first? Or do you take it off for him?"

"Dan, there's nothing between Mark and me." She could feel her stomach tying itself in knots. "How can you think there is?" Seeing him move toward her, Lisa tried to scramble off the bed, but he caught her easily.

"I saw that touching scene in the parking lot," Dan growled in her ear. His hand moved down, lingering momentarily at the sash of her robe before slowly untying it. "You've had enough men dancing to your tune long enough. Now it's your turn to dance to mine," he muttered, lowering his mouth to hers.

There was no gentleness in his kiss. Even so, Dan's hands were expert on her body, finding all the sensitive places. Lisa could feel herself falling into a sensual abyss. She knew she didn't want Dan to use her only for his own pleasure. A tear escaped her eye, then another. She didn't want her first time to be this way. Feeling the dampness on her face, Dan lifted his head, staring at her in puzzlement that soon turned to anger. "What's wrong? Aren't I as good as your other lovers?" he demanded.

"I told you—Mark and I were never lovers." Lisa felt weary. "But you don't care to believe me. What you saw was Mark kissing me good-bye. He's leaving the firm, he wanted me to come to work for him. And I refused. Of course, why should you care? For you, this is only an excuse to forcibly make love to me."

Dan's hand grasped her chin in a painful grip, forcing her to look at him. His mouth lowered to hers in another punishing kiss. Lisa lay limply, unwilling to respond to his harsh embrace. Finally, uttering a savage oath under his breath, he lifted his head and stood up, gathering his clothes together.

"Darn," Dan ground out, tucking his open shirt into his pants. "You really know how to dampen a man's enthusiasm, don't you?"

"Get out," Lisa said thickly, refusing to look up at him. She wrapped her robe around her, biting her lower lip to hold back further tears. She turned on her side, her back to him.

Dan stepped forward, his hand outstretched as if to say something, then changed his mind. A moment later, Lisa could hear the front door closing. Only then did she allow her tears to fall.

Lisa woke up Monday morning with a feeling of dread. She showered and dressed swiftly, wanting to get to the office before Dan. When she arrived at her desk, she sat down at her typewriter and inserted a sheet of stationery. With a look of determination on her face, she let her fingers fly over the keys. When she had finished, she took the sheet out of the typewriter and proofread it. After signing it, Lisa stood up and carried it into Dan's office, laying it on his desk. She had just sat down at her own desk again when Dan strode in, passing her without a word. Lisa held her breath for the space of time it would take Dan to find and read the letter.

"Lisa! Get in here!" Dan's voice cracked through the air like a whip.

She stood up, absently smoothing her skirt, and slowly walked into the inner office.

"Yes, Mr. Nolan?" she said calmly.

"What is this?" Dan waved the paper in front of her.

"My letter of resignation," Lisa said evenly.

Dan tore the paper up, tossing the scraps into the wastebasket. "No, it isn't."

"I'll just type up another one." Her gaze was unwavering.

"Why?" he demanded angrily.

"We both know the reason why, Dan," Lisa said in a low voice, not pretending to misunderstand his question. "I can't stay here."

"Yes, you can." His voice held a thread of steel. "And you will. Get your pad for dictation."

Lisa walked numbly back to her desk and picked up her steno pad. It was obvious that Dan was going to make her decision to leave as difficult as he could.

"I said I want that dictation done today, Miss Winters!" Dan barked. "Not next year."

Steeling herself not to throw the pad at Dan's head, Lisa picked up several pencils. "Coming, Mr. Nolan."

Each day was the same, with Dan sarcastically criticizing her over any tiny error in her work. And she would stand by in stony silence. There were times when she asked herself why she didn't just walk out the door and not come back. And for some reason she couldn't give herself an answer.

"This letter is totally unacceptable, Miss Winters. Try again," Dan sneered one day, dropping a crumpled ball of paper on Lisa's desk.

"Right away, Mr. Nolan," she merely murmured, inserting a fresh sheet of letterhead into the typewriter.

There were days when Lisa felt ready to scream and stamp her feet, anything to get her anger out. Instead, she stiffened her backbone and continued on. She wouldn't give Dan the satisfaction of seeing her break down in front of him.

Like clockwork, each Monday morning, Lisa left a letter of resignation on Dan's desk. Five minutes after he'd enter his office and sit at his desk, the scraps were tossed into the wastebasket without a word. Dan would then order Lisa in for dictation or to do something else, just to show her who was boss. Dan was working like a madman, and Lisa followed suit.

On the fourth Monday morning, Dan again called Lisa into his office. She had become so adept at just looking past him that she didn't notice the lines of strain about his mouth.

"You win," Dan said bleakly. "Your letter of resignation is accepted."

His words struck Lisa with the force of a hammer blow. "I'll stay until you find another secretary," she said quietly.

"No." Dan slowly shook his head. "I accept your resignation effective today. I'll have your final check for you at the end of the day."

"I see," Lisa said hoarsely. "I'll make sure to have everything caught up by then." She turned and walked woodenly back to her desk.

The day passed in a haze for Lisa. That afternoon, Dan laid a handwritten sheet in front of her. "Your letter of reference," he said gruffly. "If you'll type it up, I'll sign it."

"Thank you," she whispered, feeling tears prick the back of her eyelids.

At the end of the day, Dan called Lisa into his office and handed her an envelope. "Your check. And what will you do now?"

"I don't know. I may move back near home to be

closer to my family." And far away from you, Lisa thought painfully to herself.

Dan rubbed his eyes in a tired gesture. "I wish I knew what to say," he said finally. "I had hoped you would reconsider, but it's probably for the best."

"It is," she said, tight-lipped.

"Good-bye, Lisa." Dan's eyes were bleak as he looked at her. "The best of luck."

"Thank you," she whispered, before fleeing from the office.

Lisa was glad that she had enough savings put aside to enable her to take some time off before she began job hunting. She just didn't have any energy, and she spent her time huddled on the couch, unable to believe Dan was gone from her life for good. Tears would streak her cheeks unexpectedly during the day, and even more so at night.

"You can't keep on this way," Debra told her one day when they met for lunch. "Lee, you're a walking zombie. You have to start living again."

"I'm just allowing the wounds to heal first." Lisa smiled faintly. "Don't worry. I have a few job interviews set up for next Monday."

"I hope you look better by then." Debra eyed her critically. "I'm so sorry it all turned out this way. I honestly thought Dan would contact you after you left. I guess Xenia was wrong after all."

"I guess it was all too much to hope for." She sighed.

"Well, if you need to talk, just call me," Debra told her before they parted.

Lisa knew she couldn't talk about Dan to anyone.

Even Debra. She could only hope that going back to work would snap her out of her misery.

Lisa slept late the next day and got up feeling groggy. Looking in the mirror, she wasn't surprised to find dark circles under her eyes and hollows in her cheeks. Sighing, she went into the bathroom to take a shower. She was in the midst of drying herself off when the doorbell rang.

"Now who?" Lisa muttered to herself, grabbing her robe and wrapping it around her. Opening the front door, her eyes widened when she found a large, light brown teddy bear seated in the doorway. Lisa could feel the tears filling her eyes again as she picked up the bear and read the attached card.

If this teddy bear is allowed inside, may the other teddy bear come in too?

Lisa hugged the bear against her, beginning to cry. She knew it could only be from Dan, although the card was unsigned.

"Does that mean I can come in?" Dan's low voice sounded, hesitant.

Lisa looked up, seeing him through a misty haze. Unable to speak, she nodded, stepping back to let him pass. "I—ah—I was just getting dressed," she said huskily, composing herself. "Would you like some coffee?"

"Get dressed, and I'll fix the coffee." He disappeared into the kitchen.

Lisa went into her bedroom and closed the door behind her. She dressed in jeans and a T-shirt, then hurriedly applied her make-up with shaky fingers. When she walked back into the living room, Dan was walking out of the kitchen with two cups of coffee. He handed one to her.

"Dan, why are you here?" Lisa asked, disconcerted by the look in his eyes.

"To see you," he said simply.

Lisa bent her head, feeling a flush burn her cheeks. "Did you find a new secretary?" She sat down, curling up on the couch.

"Hired one a week ago." Dan grimaced. "She has a lot to learn. How are you doing?"

"Oh, I've been taking some time off first." She managed a shaky laugh.

"I've missed you, Lee."

His husky admission left her body trembling. "I doubt you've even noticed that I'm gone," she said.

"It's not difficult to notice when it isn't your voice answering the phone. And she doesn't have your charming habit of kicking off your shoes when you do your filing." His eyes were disturbingly intent on hers.

"I won't come back to work for you, Dan, if that's what you've come to ask," Lisa said in a low voice.

"I don't want you to." His flat statement only brought her fresh pain.

"Then why did you come here?" Lisa cried out, jumping to her feet. "*You* were the one who had been acting so indifferent when we were alone. Soon after that I wasn't sure what to think. Not *once* did you try to contact me after I left. Well, you can just take your stupid bear and go away and leave me alone!" She turned away.

Two hands gripped her shoulders, spinning her around. "You don't know how hard it was for me to keep my feelings hidden," Dan said in a low voice. "All I wanted was to make love to you. But I knew you weren't the type of woman who would be satisfied with an affair. It got harder and harder to keep my hands off you. I didn't want you to quit. And knowing your real reason for quitting didn't help. These past few weeks I have been doing a lot of serious thinking. All these years I've cast women in the same mold as my mother. It took you to make me realize that I was wrong. You could no more be like my mother than Morgan could be like you. I'm also ready to admit that you mean more to me than just being my secretary. Much more."

"You're lying." Her voice trembled.

"There were nights"—Dan's voice turned husky— "when I'd turn over in bed and reach out, dreaming you were lying beside me. But my arms only found air. Then I'd curse myself for feeling that way. And curse you for being the cause.

Lisa closed her eyes tightly, shutting out his face. His expression told her he was telling the truth.

"I apologize for that night, Lee," Dan said quietly. "I was angry and I took it out on you. I saw Connors kissing you, and I saw red. Then I got angry with myself for feeling jealous and headed for the nearest bar. The rest you know."

"What do you want, Dan? Forgiveness?" Lisa's voice rose shrilly. "After all, you only tried to rape me. Of course you're forgiven. There, does that make you feel better?" Her eyes were dark with scorn.

"No, it doesn't." Dan shook her roughly. Seeing her stricken features, his expression changed, and he pulled her into his arms. "Oh, Lee, I don't want to hurt you," Dan groaned. "I only want to love you."

"Love me?" Lisa choked back a hysterical sob. "You don't know the meaning of the word."

"I didn't used to, no. But I do now," he said thickly. "I just wasn't sure if you had any real feelings for me. Until my visitor earlier this morning." He rubbed his jaw ruefully. "Debra packs a mean whallop."

"Deb?" She looked at him with confusion.

"She stormed into my office, calling me every name in the book, saying I had ruined your life," he said wryly. "She accused me of making you fall in love with me, then callously dropping you. Then she hauled off and slapped my face—hard. Trouble is, she couldn't understand why I kissed her afterwards. She told me I was crazy. I decided I better come over here and find out for myself if it was true. Is it, Lee? Do you love me?" Dan demanded.

"It doesn't matter, Dan," she said quietly. "I'll love you until the day I die, but I can't have an affair with you, not knowing there will be a day when you'll leave me and not look back. Or that you might get it into your head that I'm like your mother after all. I just can't handle that type of pain."

"I admit there was a time when I wanted to have an affair with you. That's why I took you to see my house. I wanted to know what you'd think of living in it." Dan's fingers sensually massaged her face. "Then I started thinking of what it would be like if we raised kids there. After the car accident, I began to see how fragile and precious life can be. And that it should be enjoyed to its fullest. My feelings toward you started growing stronger, and I realized that I had to either start backing off or carry you off to my bed. Lisa, what I'm trying, very poorly, to say is that I want you to be my wife."

Lisa's head shot up in shock. "You—you want to marry me?" Her voice ended in a squeak.

"Think you could stand being married to this arrogant bully of a lawyer?" Dan smiled crookedly.

"Very much," Lisa whispered, happily linking her arms around his neck, giving herself fully to his embrace. Her fingers moved downward, unbuttoned his shirt buttons and slipped around his warm skin.

"We better get married as soon as possible," Dan muttered thickly against her lips. "Otherwise you better plan on living with me until the wedding."

"Where's that patience you're so well known for?" Lisa teased.

"I haven't been worth a plugged nickel since you left," Dan said wryly. "I'm sure Rita, my new secretary, is very happy I'm not there now. I haven't been too polite to her lately." He pulled Lisa back against him. "Now I suggest you call your parents and change your clothes, then we're going out to apply for a license and to buy you a ring. Think you can be ready in a week? That's the longest I can wait to have you."

"If you think I'm going to give you a chance to think things over and back out, you've got another think coming," Lisa teased, lifting her face and brushing her lips against his.

A week later, Lisa stood at the sliding glass door looking out at the pink-tinged sky of early morning. A man's velour robe covered her slim figure. She turned, looking at the still-sleeping figure in the bed.

"Enjoying the view?" A man's voice spoke low.

Smiling, Lisa dropped the robe to the floor and slid back into bed to warm her chilled body against Dan's warm one. "Hello, wife," he whispered against her lips. "Any regrets?"

Thinking of the pleasures Dan had shown her throughout the night, Lisa shook her head, burying her face against his neck. "None."

"You don't even feel cheated out of a big wedding?"

"I wanted you, not a wedding. You know what, Mr. Nolan? I think I love you."

Lisa could sense Dan's slow smile in the darkness. "You only think?" His hand possessively caressed her bare hip.

"I can't have you become overconfident," she said, luxuriating in the feeling of his bare skin under hers. "You're too arrogant to handle as it is."

Dan laughed deep in his throat as he pulled her beneath him. "You wouldn't have me any other way."

Her fingertips outlined his mouth. "No, I guess I wouldn't. You're all I'll ever need. For all time."

6 brand new *Silhouette Special Editions* yours for 15 days–Free!

For the reader who wants more...more story...more detail and description...more realism...and more romance...in paperback originals, 1/3 longer than our regular Silhouette Romances. Love lingers longer in new Silhouette Special Editions. Love weaves an intricate, provocative path in a third more pages than you have just enjoyed. It is love as you have always wanted it to be—and more —intriguingly depicted by your favorite Silhouette authors in the inimitable Silhouette style.

15-Day Free Trial Offer

We will send you 6 new Silhouette Special Editions to keep for 15 days absolutely free! If you decide not to keep them, send them back to us, you pay nothing. But if you enjoy them as much as we think you will, keep them and pay the invoice enclosed with your trial shipment. You will then automatically become a member of the Special Edition Book Club and receive 6 more romances every month. There is no minimum number of books to buy and you can cancel at any time.

IT'S YOUR OWN SPECIAL TIME

Contemporary romances for today's women.
Each month, six very special love stories will be yours
from SILHOUETTE. Look for them wherever books are sold
or order now from the coupon below.

$1.50 each

Hampson	☐ 1	☐ 4	☐ 16	☐ 27	Browning	☐ 12	☐ 38	☐ 53	☐ 73
	☐ 28	☐ 40	☐ 52	☐ 64 ☐ 94		☐ 93			
Stanford	☐ 6	☐ 25	☐ 35	☐ 46	Michaels	☐ 15	☐ 32	☐ 61	☐ 87
	☐ 58	☐ 88			John	☐ 17	☐ 34	☐ 57	☐ 85
Hastings	☐ 13	☐ 26	☐ 44	☐ 67	Beckman	☐ 8	☐ 37	☐ 54	☐ 72
Vitek	☐ 33	☐ 47	☐ 66	☐ 84		☐ 96			

$1.50 each

☐ 3 Powers	☐ 29 Wildman	☐ 56 Trent	☐ 79 Halldorson
☐ 5 Goforth	☐ 30 Dixon	☐ 59 Vernon	☐ 80 Stephens
☐ 7 Lewis	☐ 31 Halldorson	☐ 60 Hill	☐ 81 Roberts
☐ 9 Wilson	☐ 36 McKay	☐ 62 Hallston	☐ 82 Dailey
☐ 10 Caine	☐ 39 Sinclair	☐ 63 Brent	☐ 83 Hallston
☐ 11 Vernon	☐ 41 Owen	☐ 69 St. George	☐ 86 Adams
☐ 14 Oliver	☐ 42 Powers	☐ 70 Afton Bonds	☐ 89 James
☐ 19 Thornton	☐ 43 Robb	☐ 71 Ripy	☐ 90 Major
☐ 20 Fulford	☐ 45 Carroll	☐ 74 Trent	☐ 92 McKay
☐ 21 Richards	☐ 48 Wildman	☐ 75 Carroll	☐ 95 Wisdom
☐ 22 Stephens	☐ 49 Wisdom	☐ 76 Hardy	☐ 97 Clay
☐ 23 Edwards	☐ 50 Scott	☐ 77 Cork	☐ 98 St. George
☐ 24 Healy	☐ 55 Ladame	☐ 78 Oliver	☐ 99 Camp

$1.75 each

☐ 100 Stanford	☐ 105 Eden	☐ 110 Trent	☐ 115 John
☐ 101 Hardy	☐ 106 Dailey	☐ 111 South	☐ 116 Lindley
☐ 102 Hastings	☐ 107 Bright	☐ 112 Stanford	☐ 117 Scott
☐ 103 Cork	☐ 108 Hampson	☐ 113 Browning	☐ 118 Dailey
☐ 104 Vitek	☐ 109 Vernon	☐ 114 Michaels	☐ 119 Hampson

Silhouette Romance

15-Day Free Trial Offer
6 Silhouette Romances

6 Silhouette Romances, free for 15 days! We'll send you 6 new Silhouette Romances to keep for 15 days, absolutely free! If you decide not to keep them, send them back to us. You pay nothing.

Free Home Delivery. But if you enjoy them as much as we think you will, keep them by paying the invoice enclosed with your free trial shipment. We'll pay all shipping and handling charges. You get the convenience of Home Delivery and we pay the postage and handling charge each month.

Don't miss a copy. The Silhouette Book Club is the way to make sure you'll be able to receive every new romance we publish before they're sold out. There is no minimum number of books to buy and you can cancel at any time.

This offer expires July 31, 1982

Silhouette Book Club, Dept. SBL 17B
120 Brighton Road, Clifton, NJ 07012

Please send me 6 Silhouette Romances to keep for 15 days, absolutely free. I understand I am not obligated to join the Silhouette Book Club unless I decide to keep them.

NAME_____

ADDRESS_____

CITY_____ STATE_____ ZIP_____